Susan Wilsher lives with her husband and shaggy dog in a cosy cottage in Wales where she has had a wonderful time raising two amazing daughters.

She has thoroughly enjoyed her career as a primary teacher with a particular passion for teaching Year 6. As Literacy Co-ordinator, she found pleasure in developing language and imaginative writing with many pupils, alongside creating her own imaginary world in the clouds.

Flying abroad regularly has enhanced this project. Observations of fascinating cloud formations, shadows and reflected light have fed her imagination, leading to the development of this parallel world above our own.

For my wonderful husband, Rob; and our amazing daughters, Amy and Sammy-Jo, whose encouragement and support have helped this project reach completion.

Susan Wilsher

ZEEGLIT'S QUEST

AUSTIN MACAULEY PUBLISHERS™

LONDON · CAMBRIDGE · NEW YORK · SHARJAH

A CIP catalogue record for this title is available from the British Library.

ISBN 9781398466876 (Paperback)
ISBN 9781398466883 (ePub e-book)

www.austinmacauley.com

First Published 2023
Austin Macauley Publishers Ltd®
1 Canada Square
Canary Wharf
London
E14 5AA

I'd like to say a big thank you to the 2016/17 Y6 class of Castle Park Primary School, Caldicot for their support as we read sections of my developing text and in particular, to Jana Prelevic – an exceptionally talented young lady who has since edited my script and given me the confidence to persevere.

Table of Contents

Foreword

'Now!' whispered Zeeglit. 'Run!'

The four friends crept from the shadows and made a dash for the entrance to the gully leading away from the settlement.

It was early morning and a thin mist swirled around the Valley of Snay. Zeeglit felt his heart race along with his feet as he neared the bend that would take them from the sight of the elders – those same elders who had always told tales to frighten young moogles from taking the path along the steep-sided valley they were now entering. Tales of some strange sounding outcast living in a clearing shrouded in mystery and fear.

'Wait. Let's see if we've been noticed,' said Noo-Noo, Zeeglit's younger sister by just a year.

Once round the bend, there was no sight of home and no sounds of anyone following so the four youngsters began to turn their attention to what lay ahead. The valley appeared to become steeper and narrower as it led away from the gently rolling landscape of home.

This was an adventure the friends had been planning for a while and the excitement was clear in their eyes. The obvious way forward was the centre of the valley floor so, with Zeeglit leading the way, they set off.

'How far do you think it is?' asked Groo, a short, dark-furred moogle with a permanently worried expression.

'I don't think it's very far,' answered Zeeglit confidently. 'I heard one of the elders say that they had been there and back between sunrise and sunset. They claim to have had their fortune told by the seer.'

'It's all rubbish if you ask me,' said Filla, the other female of the group as shown by the light streak of fur running from the top of her head, all the way down her back. 'I'm only here to prove its nonsense.'

Making their way along what was a surprisingly easy path, the four friends chattered on for a while. Around late morning they stopped for a quick snack from some particularly fresh-looking floss shrubs. Taking stock of their surroundings, Zeeglit noticed a slight change in the colour of the scree they were now sitting on and he was sure the temperature was dropping despite the sun now being high in the sky.

As they stood to move on, it was obvious the others had also noticed changes as they began to talk in whispers and cast anxious glances to the side and behind. Walking close together, Groo had just suggested turning round for the third time when Zeeglit put up his hand and they all stopped.

A little way ahead, they could see a cluster of bushes on each side of the path with a gap between and an arch above. This had definitely been created by someone and Zeeglit had a feeling they had reached their destination.

In silence now, Zeeglit again led the way forward, keeping to one side of the path and walking as quietly as possible.

A wavering whisper of 'I really think we should go back now' came from the back of the group quickly followed by a firm 'no' from Zeeglit. 'This is what we came to see.'

As they reached the gateway, Zeeglit motioned for the others to stay back and crouching down, he peered around the shrubbery. The sight that met his eyes was unlike anything he'd seen before and it took him a while to take it in.

A high rocky bank enclosed a perfect circle of land. Tall stone pillars had been erected in the centre of the clearing, making a smaller circle with one flat, circular stone in the centre. At one side was a strange domed structure created from a mound of white stones – particularly striking against the shiny black floor of the entire amphitheatre.

There appeared to be an opening at the front of the dome and strange bare trees stood like soldiers between this building and the central circle. Light-reflecting discs hung from every available branch and bounced sunlight around the area in a dazzling display.

As nobody seemed to be about, Zeeglit motioned for his friends to follow and they crept stealthily through the arch. Open-mouthed, the four young moogles stood and looked around in awe muttering phrases like,

'Wow!'

'What is this place?'

'I don't think we should be here!' (The latter from Groo, unsurprisingly!)

Keeping a wary eye on the white mound, they walked towards the centre of the arena with rainbow lights dancing around them.

Noo-Noo reached the circular stone first and jumped onto its centre, raising both arms victoriously. However, her victory was short-lived as the stone began to shake and slowly rise into the air.

'Jump off! Quick!' shouted Zeeglit but Noo-Noo, too terrified to move, sank to her knees and waited for it to stop.

Higher and higher the pillar grew until there was no way she could get down. With all eyes trained on Noo-Noo, no one noticed the strange creature that had emerged from the entrance to the stone dwelling and was making its slow but steady way between the trees towards the inner circle.

'Well, well! What do we have here?' asked a deep, mellow voice just behind Filla.

Spinning around, the youngsters were shocked to see a tall creature draped in uneven black rags that formed a thick cloak, complete with a hood which was pulled forward covering its face.

Zeeglit took a second to realise the newcomer didn't look angry and stepped forward.

'We're sorry if we've disturbed you but we've travelled from The Valley of Snay and our friend is stuck on your pillar.'

'I can see that, young Zeeglit. I have been awaiting your arrival. Follow me.' And turning without a glance at Noo-Noo, he began to make his way slowly back past the trees.

'Hey, wait! How do you know my name? What do you mean you've been waiting for me? And what about my sister?'

Pausing to turn back, the creature said, 'Come. She'll be fine.'

Motioning the other two friends to wait by the pillar, Zeeglit hurried to catch up with the cloaked figure just as he reached the entrance to the dome.

'Come in, come in. You will suffer no harm,' said the mellow voice leading the way into the gloom.

Following carefully, Zeeglit took a few steps into the dome and stood still as his eyes grew accustomed to the darkness. Subtle lighting came from a hanging glow lamp in the centre of the circular room and gradually he was able to see more of his strange surroundings.

Though unlike anywhere Zeeglit had seen before, the room had a very comfortable feeling. A stone ledge ran round the whole perimeter and was cluttered with all manner of things: a collection of clear jars containing what looked like strange seeds and fruits, a pile of colourful boxes and a strange blue and green orb on a stand that Zeeglit would have loved to take a closer look at.

However, the seer, for that's who it must surely be, was clearing a table underneath the lamp and gestured to Zeeglit to take a seat on the floor cushion a few steps away. Keeping his eyes fixed on his host; Zeeglit did so and watched as the cloak was removed to reveal a very strange creature indeed.

Long, fine silver hair hung to middle of a back clothed in a loose robe of black fibres of a type the young moogle was not familiar with. This swished as the slim figure turned and a pair of large hazel eyes with elongated black pupils twinkled in Zeeglit's direction.

'Call me Valish. Does anyone know you are here?' he asked as he settled himself in a similar cushion on the opposite side of the table, crossing long, thin legs and resting surprisingly bald arms on the table.

'No one. But I suppose you already know that if you can see everything!'

'There's no need to be sarcastic, young Zeeglit. I was just making conversation. Now, tell me: what did you hope to gain from coming here?'

'Well, I guess we were curious.' Zeeglit paused to consider. 'Can you really see into the future?'

'That I can, young moogle. I suppose you want to know about your future?'

Zeeglit nodded.

'Your future is an interesting one – not least because all is not clear to me. I can usually see what path a life will take but in your case that's not so. I have had dreams recently where I saw you and heard your name. I know you are destined to lead an important life and this will not be the only adventure you will undertake.'

'Is there anything that is clear?' asked a fascinated Zeeglit.

'Travel is definitely part of the plan.' There is a prophecy that has been handed down through time:

'An evil descends from the heavens
On the back of a fallen star,
Only the hands of a healer
Can vanquish these woes from afar.'

'I believe that may involve you but more than that I cannot say.'

'Can't say or won't say?' Zeeglit questioned, now sitting on the front of his cushion, his eyes glued to Valish.

'I can't say because I can only catch glimpses and these are of things so strange, I am unable to put them into words. I can tell you that you will see things none of your folk have ever seen before and there will be danger along the way.'

'My father is a healer but not me,' said Zeeglit thoughtfully.

'You are yet young,' returned Valish as he stood. 'Now, come, young Zeeglit. Let's go and get your sister down from her prison.'

And before Zeeglit could ask anything further, the seer led the way back into the sunlight.

Chapter 1
The Journey Begins

Moogles have inhabited the cloud-lands since the beginning of time. Gentle, peaceful creatures standing, on average, a little under a metre tall, they can live for several hundred years.

This particular morning had started like most others in the Valley of Snay on the Nimbostratus: the lowest of the cloud layers. Augil and her oldest child, Zeeglit: a lively, adventurous twelve-year old, had gone to gather enough food for the family.

It is unusual for a moogle to eat more than one meal in a day as their tummies are small and the food extremely nutritious. Their diet consists almost entirely of nimbo-tuft: a nourishing shrub that grows easily with long, narrow strips that hang in clusters: some white; some grey; some silver, and can be eaten straight from the plant. Growing freely, it's easy to gather enough to feed a family and the moogles living in the Valley of Snay had a fine patch of shrubs growing close by.

Chattering about this and that, mother and son made their way to a patch of tuft and Zeeglit reached out to pluck a handful.

'Oh!' he exclaimed. 'Look, Ma. I don't fancy this.'

Augil moved to look at the shrub Zeeglit was holding and had to admit that she had never seen a plant look less appetising. This tuft was beginning to curl at the tips and the colour had faded to a dull shade of grey. 'I'm sure it's nothing to worry about,' she replied and she turned away to look at the other plants growing nearby. They quickly realised that it wasn't the only one in the area with a problem but they managed to pick enough healthy nimbo-tuft for their evening meal.

Chatting about what they had seen and carrying their harvest in nets slung over their shoulders, they made their way back home. Moogles live in clusters; some large, some small, making their family homes in burrows scooped out of the floss, the moogle name for the cloud mass.

Later, as they sat down to eat, Zeeglit heard his mother talking to his father, Ressa, about the plants but the meal tasted the same as usual and he forgot all about it – until the following day. Making their way back to the same area as the day before, they could see that the leaves had curled even more and the shrubs were looking rather lifeless.

Wandering around the area where many other shrubs grew, they were very concerned to see that they were all looking similar and when they bumped into one of their neighbours on the way home, they learnt that other plants in the area were affected in the same way.

The following day, a meeting was held in the valley and many moogles attended, all reporting the same thing. Several of the younger moogles had walked quite a distance in all directions from Snay and the story was the same everywhere they had looked. The elders couldn't remember anything like this in the past and no one could suggest a reason for it happening now. As the meeting broke up and families made their way home, Ressa stayed behind with a few of his oldest friends.

'You go ahead and get the youngsters to bed,' he said to Augil. 'We want to talk further to see if we can find a solution. I'll be home soon.'

Zeeglit noticed his mother was unusually quiet as they walked slowly home with his three siblings: Noo-Noo, his younger sister by a year, Blin, a cheeky chap aged four and Exie, the baby at almost two. Safely tucked in the family burrow, Zeeglit was almost asleep in his comfortable nest when his father finally arrived home. He could tell by the way his parents talked that they were very worried.

'Do you know why?' Augil asked sleepily.

'No idea,' Ressa replied. 'It's a total mystery. The growing conditions have been good and there is no sign of pollution. So far, it doesn't seem to be making anyone ill but I'm not sure how nourishing it is and if it continues like this, it won't be long before it's not edible. A group is going to set off at first light to find a healthy crop and gather enough for a couple of months but I'm quite worried.' This, in turn, made Zeeglit really worried as nothing usually bothered his father.

Over the next few days, the condition of the plants slowly got worse and it became tasteless and rather chewy. The search party returned with a good supply of healthy tuft which was put into store as it lasts for a while, but they'd had to travel for a full day before they had reached an area where the shrubs seemed unaffected.

More meetings were held and search parties went off again in the hopes of filling a store to cover the next few months if things got worse. It made Zeeglit nervous to see the usually carefree creatures around him become increasingly serious.

For a while, they worried about the problem until one morning Ressa made a surprising announcement:

'I'm thinking about travelling to the high-level Cirrostratus my father told me about when I was a lad. There, the great plains of ice-cirrus grow and I can bring enough back to feed us for a while.'

Due to the strong sunlight on top of the Cirrostratus, combined with the ice crystals within the clouds, the perfect conditions exist for cirro-tuft bushes to grow. These rare silver shrubs reportedly produce clusters of sparkly strands of the most delicious food imaginable. Ressa had told him about the way *his* father's eyes had glazed over when he described having once tasted the rare food as a boy – a taste few moogles could claim to have savoured.

Even more importantly, the crop was extremely nourishing and a tiny amount could sustain a moogle for a few days. However, the long journey there, with hazards along the way, made it a trip very few moogles had made, or at least returned from, and Augil worried when she realised where his thoughts were leading.

Despite the temptations, Ressa's father had never made the dangerous journey to the higher plains and had always warned his sons against doing so. He had told of many hazards to be overcome along the way and the likelihood of coming across a member of the notorious thordite clan was enough to stop most moogles from attempting the adventure. These warriors of the skies are known for their aggressive strength and power but, thankfully, live mainly in dark areas of clouds away from moogle settlements.

Zeeglit could tell that his father was seriously worried and he knew something had to be done. He had always been ready to rise to a challenge and he felt his blood begin to fizz with excitement as an idea crept into his mind. He listened to his parents talk for most of the day until Ressa mentioned that he wouldn't be able to carry much. Zeeglit couldn't wait any longer.

'I'll come with you! I can carry some too.'

'No, Zeeglit,' Ressa replied, without even looking his way.

'It's out of the question!' answered Augil at the same time. 'It's far too dangerous.'

'I'd be so careful and only do what I was told,' Zeeglit pleaded.

But the answer stayed the same.

Ressa also explained that it was possible that he would find the answer to their current problem if he travelled via the Altostratus, the level above their homeland. He could find out if they were having the same problem with their plants and if they knew why.

The final straw came as they sat down to a meal of limp, sour-tasting tuft and they all knew that the time had come. Later that evening, whilst sitting in the entrance to their burrow, Zeeglit heard his father tell Augil of his decision to travel to the higher plains.

'But why you?' questioned Augil, her warm tones rippling softly through the dusk. 'I'm sure the problem with the tuft won't last and someone younger could go. We can live off the supply in the store for a while and the plants growing here will probably be better by then.'

'We can live like that for a few months but I have a bad feeling that it's not just going to go away. If I set off now, I know you will have enough to eat for a while. Its many moons now since I last went travelling and I've always wanted the best for my family. We need to find the reason behind the failure of the crop for the future of our family and friends.' Reaching out to stroke her face, he added in a lighter tone, 'And I want to see the look in your eyes as you taste something more wonderful than you can yet imagine.'

Slowly, steadily, Ressa's voice flowed over Augil like treacle off a warm spoon and she knew that, despite her pleading, he would make preparations for the adventure ahead. And it was there and then that Zeeglit made his plan!

Pretending to be asleep, he watched his father pack as little as he thought he could get away with: one change of waistcoat; a collecting net for the ice-cirrus, his dimometer (an ancient directional aid handed down through the generations) and a gantate or lantern in case of fog or poor visibility. Once he was sure his father was asleep, Zeeglit crept from his bed, took his own collecting net, food and ice-board and, leaving a quickly scribbled note on his nest, he slipped silently out of the burrow.

During the misty light of early morning the following day, long before his family and friends were up and about, Ressa put his pack on his back and took a long look at his home before turning to stride off through the Burrows of Snay. Waiting in the shadows close by, Zeeglit spotted him leave and began to follow at a safe distance until they were too far from home for him to be sent back.

Ressa's aim was to reach Glim in the Valley of Quaron by nightfall in the hope of catching a clear moonbeam to the highest level. These rays of pure moonlight contain a central column of air moving in either an upward or downward direction.

By midday, they had walked many kilometres, as moogles move surprisingly quickly for their size, and Ressa pulled off a handful of healthy nimbo-tuft to eat as he rested against the soft cushion of his pack. Zeeglit decided that this was his moment and waited for his father's anger as he walked up to join him. However, far from being surprised, Ressa patted the ground next to him:

'I thought I might see you here,' he said, handing a small clump of tuft to his son.

'How?'

'When I was your age, I would have done the same thing and you are a lot like me. Does your mother know?'

'I left a note.'

And that was it. Father and son sat together sharing a simple meal while Ressa told him of his plan.

Zeeglit must have dozed off because he was suddenly jolted awake by a crowd of young moogles cloud-surfing past where he sat. Without thinking, he was on his feet and grabbing his ice-board.

'Hey!'

The group of five youngsters of his own age turned at his shout and he raced over to them. After a quick introduction, one of the group, Keeta, explained that he had a new board and they were going to see what it could do. Made from pure, strengthened ice, the boards are polished to a high shine to make them fast and this new board was of the latest design with a higher curve at the front.

They were close to the local arena: a space where the floss dipped and rose to make an exciting course for surfing, the main runs shining with use, and always a popular place to be. With a quick word to Ressa, Zeeglit joined them for a very happy hour and he was impressed as Keeta took the board to the highest ramp. Giving it a strong push, he quickly jumped on, bent his knees and elbows to balance and steer and he was off. Using his own board, Zeeglit joined in the fun and Keeta even let him try his board. It took a while to get used to the new angle but it gave an exciting ride and he was sad when the time came to leave.

Ressa climbed to his feet as Zeeglit reappeared and, glancing quickly at his dimometer, they set off westwards. Taking in the sights and sounds and feeling a sense of purpose, Zeeglit enjoyed the walk and by evening on that first day, they had covered a pleasing distance, arriving at Glim shortly before nightfall. There, many moogles were gathering for the nightly transportation – Glim being one of the busiest ports for moonbeam travel in the area.

Walking between the entrances to communal burrows known as "stay-by's" where travellers could get a night's rest, they made their way towards the transit depot. Zeeglit had heard about these places before and he stayed close to his father.

Ressa chatted with a group of elders gathered nearby, all of whom were travelling to the Alto Level. He felt it best not to mention his intended destination as he knew the elders would think him foolish and try to dissuade him from his upward journey, so he merely said he was travelling higher to get a better view of the Oodle Pool (the moogles name for Earth), as it was known to become clearer as you travelled higher.

He did take the opportunity to ask them about the tuft growing in their homelands. But none of them had heard of the problem he described. Feeling relieved that it was not yet widespread; Ressa took Zeeglit under an impressive grey archway marking one of the entrances to the depot. It seemed a good place to rest for a couple of hours before moonlight so the pair settled down and Zeeglit was soon asleep.

Opening his eyes, Zeeglit could see that night was now fully in place and the moon was making an appearance so he stood by Ressa as they moved into the transit area. It was now much busier and moogles of all shapes and sizes milled around: families with excited youngsters tried to keep together; moogles travelling this way for the first time hung back apprehensively whilst seasoned travellers strode confidently to the front.

Luckily, it was a clear night and as the first beams appeared, moogles began to gather near the shafts. The transit zone was marked by a circular structure of tall wide arches with a smooth, shiny floor trampled by thousands of moogles passing through over the years. The platform was wide but the end was abrupt and quite alarming as it represented the edge of a void where it was known that some of the strongest moonbeams passed by. As the moon rose higher in the sky, the beams became clearer and when a strong, bright column of light passed close to the platform, a traveller would leap into the centre and begin their journey. Generally, moogles travelled alone but if it was a strong shaft, there was just enough room for an adult and child together. Gradually, individuals chose their own ray of light and those left behind became fewer in number.

Zeeglit had not travelled this way before and he was very nervous as his time came and they made their way to the front of the platform. As their turn approached, he prepared himself for moonbeam entry as Ressa had told him. He waited for Ressa's shout then, holding his breath and his father's paws, he jumped into a particularly strong shaft of moonlight and felt his legs weaken with the upward thrust. Holding onto Ressa's fur and keeping his legs a little distance apart to balance, he soon adjusted to the ride. The feeling of speed was like nothing he had ever felt and he gave a whoop of sheer joy as he shot upwards like a rocket.

After half an hour or so, Zeeglit was becoming accustomed to the steady upward movement and was beginning to feel more relaxed. His view beyond the shaft was limited by the bright light of the beam but around him he was delighted to see the colourful light-flies zipping about; the tail of each, glowing in brightly to create a rainbow of colours. These harmless and entertaining bugs entered and left the shaft at their will; recharging their tiny tail lights with the power of the moonbeams.

Now the use of moonbeams is a very fast and exciting method of travel but it does come with danger as the moonbeams cross the Whizz-pod Zone! Most whizz-pods (or aeroplanes to you and I) travel during daylight hours but it is the night flights that cause havoc for some travelling moogles. The journey to the Alto Level usually took a couple of hours, and then it was another couple to the Cirrus.

Zeeglit was so absorbed, watching the light-flies, that a jolt in his airflow caused him to lose his balance and, for a moment, he was scared of being thrown out of the shaft between levels.

'Hold on!' yelled his father and feeling firm paws supporting him, he had just managed to steady himself when there was a second jolt; this time accompanied by a loud roaring noise.

There was no time to think; Zeeglit struggled to maintain his balance as the shaft wavered and fear raced through him. Beyond the shaft wall, he was horrified to make out the shape of a huge roaring monster with a row of glowing eyes as it passed alarmingly close to his moonbeam.

Time seemed to slow down as the shaft he was travelling in bucked and shuddered and the air was filled with the deafening roar. Our terrified moogles thought the end had come!

In a few short seconds, the roar had faded to a distant rumble and the moonbeam steadied. However, Zeeglit felt far from steady! He was relieved when they reached the Alto Level and Ressa lifted him and jumped from the shaft to make an overnight stay they hadn't been prepared for. He could see that his father was also shaken and they sank down on the platform together as their unsteady legs gave way and Zeeglit felt himself begin to tremble with the after effect of the shock.

'Are you alright?' Ressa asked, looking far from alright himself.

'I think so, but what was that?'

'That was a whizz pod: a creature from the Oodle Pool. I'm sorry you had to see that but it's never happened to me before. I think we'll stay here for the night.'

As Ressa took hold of his paw to lead him from the platform, Zeeglit realised the encounter would stay with him for ever and he thought about how lucky they had been.

Chapter 2
A Night's Rest

As they moved through the station on the middle cloud layer, all around was chaos. Officials were rushing around checking everyone was ok and newcomers were prevented from travelling. Tearful travellers worried about what might have been and there was a buzz of conversation as moogles discussed the disruption to many of the light shafts as the whizz-pod had roared unexpectedly by. Several concerned moogles came to check Ressa and Zeeglit were alright but Ressa assured them they just wanted some time to enjoy the feel of the solid ground beneath them.

By listening to conversations around them, they learnt that regular service had been discontinued until further notice as officials tried to understand this unexpected event and predict the chances of it being a big problem or a one-off occurrence.

Feeling steadier, father and son had just stood to leave when they walked past a small group of officials gathered around an elderly moogle lying on the ground. Motioning for Zeeglit to wait a moment, Ressa moved closer.

'Can I ask what the problem is? I may be able to help,' he said.

'This elder was shaken about in his shaft during the disruption and is feeling quite unwell,' answered the official nearest the edge of the group.

'May I?' asked Ressa and he bent down next to the prone figure. 'Hi-lo, friend. Where do feel discomfort?'

Lifting his paw to his chest, the elder whispered, 'Here.'

Gently, Ressa laid his paws on the elder's chest and felt the familiar warmth that came with healing – a gift he had inherited from his father. As the heat died away, Ressa removed his paws and helped the other moogle to sit.

'Thank you, friend. I feel much better now.'

Leaving his patient in the caring hands of the officials, Ressa returned to an impressed Zeeglit and they moved out of the station.

'I know I have seen it before but how does it feel to do that?' Zeeglit asked his father.

'It feels good. To be able to help others is always rewarding. One day you may know as I feel sure you will inherit the gift. Time will tell. Now, let's find somewhere to rest.'

Ressa had not expected to spend the night in this area, so he began to look around for a place to stay. When travelling, moogles often use their large, leathery paws to dig a shallow burrow for the night, but in areas where many moogles gather, such as moonbeam ports, there are usually places to stop for the night.

These stay-by's vary in style and size and, in turn for a night's rest, all visitors must perform some sort of task to benefit the accommodation, i.e., tidying, digging a new chamber, entertaining other guests, etc., as there is no system of money on the stratus.

As many others were also faced with a disruption to their journey, the stay-by's nearest the port were very busy so the pair wandered a short way off, towards a doorway marked with an intriguing, bright banner.

Drawing closer, Zeeglit touched the gently flapping material which was smooth to the touch; silvery on one side and bright red with an unusual design in yellow and gold on the other:

'Hi lo, travellers. Are you looking to stay by the port tonight?'

A cheerful moogle of a similar age to Ressa appeared from the entrance next to the banner and Zeeglit felt relieved to be greeted by such a friendly individual.

'It's certainly busy out here tonight,' remarked the owner of the stay-by as he glanced around. 'Have I missed something?'

'You could say that,' replied Ressa and he proceeded to tell the tale of the whizz-pod and their recent close encounter.

'Well, well! You could certainly do with a comfy place to unwind. I'm Boolog. Come in, come in,' and he turned to lift a lilac lamp from a shelf alongside the entrance. (Moogle burrows are lit by glow-worms housed in crystal lamps to enhance their glow. These magical creatures come in all the colours of the rainbow and enhance the mood of a room by casting light of a chosen colour.)

Boolog led the way down a gradually sloping tunnel lit by a mixture of red and yellow lamps giving an overall orange glow – very warm and welcoming. This opened out into a large central area with Moogles of varying ages sitting around and chatting or playing games on comfortable cushions of dried floss. This chamber had the same welcoming glow and was a similar structure to many Moogle dwellings, with a sunken central area surrounded by a walkway and openings to other pods leading off around the perimeter.

Looking up to see the new arrival, one character of forty years or so, dressed in a striking silver waistcoat, spoke out:

'You are out and about late. Have you travelled far?' The others stopped what they were doing.

'Friends, our new arrivals have a story to tell of great drama and excitement. What say you that we let them refresh themselves then tell us all the tale of his night's adventures in return for their stay?' suggested the owner.

This idea was greeted with great enthusiasm as Moogles just love a good story.

'That sounds very exciting. I'm Galvees, by the way. Would you be happy to do that?' asked the owner of the silver waistcoat and Ressa, though tired, agreed, feeling that to talk through the night's events might help him to come to terms with what had happened.

Following Boolog, they were led down one of many short tunnels leading from the central chamber into a small but adequate sleeping pod. Hanging the lilac lamp from a hook on the wall, the owner turned to go.

'When you are ready, come back through and I will have a dish of ice-nip ready for you to steady yourself.'

'Thank you for your kindness. That sounds good,' replied Ressa gratefully.

'Are you happy to join the group? You can sleep here if you'd prefer,' asked Ressa.

In the centre of the chamber, a large nest of soft, dry grass beckoned temptingly but Zeeglit quickly decided that if he lay down, he would just sleep until morning and miss this new experience of a stay-by so, with a deep sigh, he shook his head, put down his pack and followed his father back to the central chamber.

A place had been prepared for them at the head of the circle of guests and shortly after they had relaxed onto the waiting cushions of floss, Boolog appeared with the promised refreshment for Ressa and a cup of dew for Zeeglit.

This dish of ice-nip, Ressa was pleased to note as he took it from his host, was of a perfect temperature and he took a small sip before looking round at the other guests.

To his right sat the youngest of the group: female twins of about Zeeglit's age, each dressed in pale blue tunics and playing the popular game of Pendra. Carefully, they took it in turns to arrange chips of hard, black root, dug from below the Bru-glit shrubs to form a pyramid (the winner being the one who can balance the most chips in a wigwam structure without it collapsing).

Next to the twins sat their parents: a pleasant looking couple who smiled in welcome, and an elderly moogle, much older than Zeeglit, who nodded his head in sleep, making gentle wheezing sounds and dribbling from one corner of his mouth.

Galvees, the friendly individual from earlier, was sat next to two females of a similar age who, Zeeglit later learned, were his sisters. These three had fur of the palest grey, flecked with pure white, usually found on moogles from the Cirrostratus and Ressa made a mental note to ask them about his intended destination at some point during his stay.

The final members of the circle were Boolog, the host, who sat to Zeeglit's right, very happy amongst his gathering of guests, and a rather rotund male of middle years with a jolly face and a rather brightly coloured waistcoat, who sat sucking silently on a poplic stem: a long grass with a hollow centre filled with a sweet, honey-type liquid taken to ease digestion.

'Hi lo,' began Ressa as a hush fell over the group and everyone turned expectantly towards him. 'We had not intended to break our journey here tonight, but circumstances beyond my control and beyond my great years of experience have caused me to change my plans.'

The twins settled themselves on their tummies, chins resting on their paws, and Ressa began to retell the story of the night's adventures, making sure to include all the details from waiting for a suitable moonbeam, to the enchanting fireflies and then the terrifying encounter with the whizz-pod.

The audience gave gasps of delight then expressions of horror as the story unfolded. The twin's eyes grew wide with astonishment and, when Ressa eventually finished his tale, there was a short period of silence then everyone began to speak at once.

There were many questions to answer and the event was discussed in great detail: most of the adults questioning what this might mean and for several, giving rise to concerns that their journeys may be changed by this event.

Ressa learned that the family with the twins were due to travel down to the Nimbo-stratus to visit relatives the following night and he felt rather guilty as he realised his tale had made the youngsters feel anxious about their intended journey.

Finally, much later than he had imagined, Ressa bid his companions good night and carried a sleeping Zeeglit back to his pod where the restful lilac hue cast by the glow-worm lamp made the sleeping chamber particularly inviting. Stopping only to remove his waistcoat, he flopped onto his comfortable nest and was instantly asleep.

When he awoke next morning, Zeeglit wondered where he was for a second then his memory came flooding back. He was alone in the pod so, keen to hear the latest news, he scrambled to his feet. No one was in the central chamber as he passed through but he could hear voices coming from outside.

Blinking in the brightness, he was surprised to see the sun was high in the sky and shadows cast by the undulating cloud masses were short. Ressa was standing under the banner with the owner of the stay-by, talking to a small group about the drama of the previous night. Zeeglit scampered over and listened for a few moments but it seemed that but no-one had any new information to offer.

'Come back inside for refreshment before you make your way,' offered Boolog.

'Thank you. I am quite hungry now you mention it,' replied Ressa and, bidding goodbye to the others, they made their way back inside and Boolog disappeared off into the kitchen pod.

'How did you sleep?' asked Ressa as they made themselves comfortable in the central chamber.

'So good I forgot where I was when I woke up!' answered Zeeglit as Galvees entered, still wearing the striking silver waistcoat from the night before.

'Ah, hi-lo, friends. Did you sleep well?' he enquired, settling down opposite Zeeglit.

'We certainly did, thank you and I am glad to have the chance to speak to you before we leave. Am I right in thinking you are from the Cirrostratus?'

'Yes, you are. Have you ever been there?'

'Well, no, but that's where we were heading last night when our journey was interrupted,' answered Ressa. 'We're hoping to go there to gather some of the ice-cirrus to take back home, as the food in our valley has become poor. Many years ago, my father told me of the delicacy grown on your level and I want to try it.'

'It is true that the cirro-tuft is quite something and a little certainly goes a long way. However, there are dangers to be faced when travelling on the upper layer.'

'I have heard that. I believe that's why so few have visited yet I feel the challenge is worth it. What can you tell me to make my journey easier?'

Galvees spent a moment thinking before announcing, 'The main thing to watch for is the shifting floss. You can never be sure of the ground beneath your feet and many have fallen to a sorry end. There is nothing you can do to prevent this and I strongly advise someone of your years to think again. Someone younger may be more agile and able to jump away from danger.'

Ressa, a little offended by reference to his age, decided to ignore this comment. 'Where would you recommend looking for the best crop?'

'You would find the shrubs growing in many areas and all are similar quality. It is the high altitude that makes for the best flavour and that is the same all over.'

With that, Boolog bustled back into the chamber with food for three.

'I thought I heard you arrive. I've prepared a snack for you as your sisters ate earlier.' And he presented the guests with a dish of food each.

A quick breakfast of alto-tuft made a tasty change to the nimbo-tuft eaten at home. Waiting until Zeeglit had eaten a little, Ressa asked.

'Do you like it?'

'Yes, it looks the same but it tastes quite different,' replied Zeeglit, enjoying the flavour.

'As the cloud levels become higher, so the air becomes thinner and it causes the shrubs growing on each higher level to be lighter and more succulent than the layer below,' explained Ressa. 'You wait until you try the ice-cirrus!'

This helped to remind Ressa of the purpose of his journey and he was eager to be on his way. Gathering their belongings and saying goodbye to Boolog and Galvees, father and son once again walked back into the daylight.

Chapter 3
The Magic of a Wedding

Steadying his pack on his back, Ressa explained that they would begin by returning to the area of their arrival the previous night; just to check there was no chance of the port being reopened by evening and if not, find the direction of the nearest alternative.

It was a lovely bright morning and many moogles who would normally have been going about their daily business were today huddled together reviewing the previous night's events. One moogle who had spoken to Ressa and Zeeglit in the transit zone the previous evening, called over to ask how they were and he stopped for a while to chat before going on his way and they continued past other stay-by's with strange relics hanging outside.

These were the markers you looked for if you wanted a room for the night and they were often very random indeed. The signs were made from bits and pieces that had blown onto the cloud layers from other lands and were very mysterious to the simple moogles. Over the years, Ressa had seen various scraps of fabrics he was unfamiliar with, thin strips of rubber that someone had once told him was called a balloon, small metal pieces hung on rope and various other things.

When they reached the scene of last night's incident, they quickly discovered that events had been more serious than they'd realised.

The whizz-pod had cut through two shafts which had luckily been empty at the time. However, this made the event extremely serious and there was no doubt that normal service would not be continued for some time at least.

Ressa could see a moon-shaft officer at the centre of a crowd of other travellers so they made their way over to hear what was being said.

Most moogles were interested in travelling down to the Nimbostratus but it appeared that the port of Pobble, several days trek to the east would be Ressa and Zeeglit's best chance of catching a moonbeam up to their intended level.

Ressa was disappointed to add this delay to the length of his time away from his family, yet he was quite glad to have a little time before he had to climb back into a light shaft as his encounter the previous night had upset him more than he'd first realised, although he tried not to let Zeeglit see this.

Ressa explained the plan to Zeeglit as they stepped back into the sunlight and set off in the direction they'd been told. As they walked briskly on their way, Zeeglit enjoyed the view around him. The scenery on this Alto Level was quite different to below and, as it was his first visit here, there was much to look at.

Whilst being formed mainly of water droplets, as on his home level, the appearance of occasional ice crystals added a sparkle to everything and the glimpses of the Oodle Pool looked particularly blue far, far below.

Towards late afternoon, they passed an area where young moogles had been out and about creating interesting shapes in the vapour; shapes that fascinate humans living on the Oodle Pool as they look up on bright yet cloudy days.

This favourite pastime of young moogles was something Zeeglit had always enjoyed as they could use their imagination and creativity to mould wonderful shapes before casting them adrift from the main body of vapour to drift clearly across the blue before gradually being diffused by the wind.

The images they choose are always of objects they have heard about but never seen. It is rumoured that some moogle many, many years ago had visited the Oodle Pool and brought back a collection of illustrations of objects common on that planet. These strange things are a fascination for moogles and are handed down from one generation to the next. Parents draw sketches of them on the floss and youngsters mould them and send them on their way.

'This would be a good time for a break,' suggested Ressa and Zeeglit was very happy to stop and watch for a while. They wondered about some of the unfamiliar objects from another world, before setting off again towards Pobble.

It was one of those days when the layers of stratus seem to deepen and merge; confusing the eye as you look towards the horizon and the journey seemed endless. Ressa kept a close eye on the directions shown on his dimometer. This bronze orb clicked open to reveal a surprisingly blue interior with a suspended arrow which pointed to the magnetic north. Zeeglit had always marvelled at how it stayed central to the orb without being attached anywhere but Ressa had explained that there was a magnetic force field within the instrument and this gave a very accurate reading of direction.

As the daylight began to fade, Ressa was pleased with how far they'd come. He was also feeling very tired, having taken a lot more exercise than he had for ages and, aware that Zeeglit had slowed down, he was keen to find somewhere to rest.

Nightfall saw them near a cluster of burrows owned by a small but very friendly clan of moogles. They were invited to shelter in one of their burrows that was currently empty, thus saving Ressa the effort of digging his own and providing some good company for the hours before bed. It didn't take them long to get to sleep and in no time at all, it was morning.

Feeling a lot more positive after a good night's sleep, Ressa woke Zeeglit and they made their way outside where it was a glorious day and the horizon looked clear and bright. A quick roll in the morning dew helped to freshen up their fur and after a short grooming session and a brief farewell, they were on their way.

Up and down they went, following a well-trodden path over mounds of dense floss. In some places, a platform of pale grey stretched out before them, whilst in others they would descend into a shady valley before climbing back out into the sunshine.

After one particularly cold, dark area, Zeeglit felt the relief of climbing up to be bathed in the warmth of the golden sunlight. However, the pleasure was short-lived as he turned his eyes westwards. He felt his spirits drop as the floss in front of them became fragmented and he realised they were going to have to cross an area of jumping stones: a part of the journey he had not thought about but which may have put him off coming.

This phenomenon sometimes occurs above the great expanses of water way below on the Oodle Pool. In these areas, the stratus often breaks up into tiny islands that sail slowly across the blue expanse carried by the currents of air. To cross these areas, it is necessary to catch a tiny fragment of cloud as it sails across the wide open area; ready to jump from one to another as two collide and then move on.

Now, there were not many things that really bothered Zeeglit as he was a plucky youth but, ever since he was little, Zeeglit had been terrified of water. He didn't really know why: his regular roll in the dew to refresh his fur was not a problem for him but, on the rare occasion he had seen a pool of gathered water, he felt himself break out in a sweat and would back away from the edge.

'Don't worry; it will be fine,' said Ressa, realising how Zeeglit was feeling but as he stood and watched the scene before him, Zeeglit felt particularly vulnerable as the cloudlets were so small and the expanse of water way below was so huge. He felt his palms begin to sweat and his chest tighten.

'Can we go around?' he asked quietly.

'No, we would have to go a very long way to avoid this area and we really have no choice.'

Standing close to Ressa, Zeeglit watched the area in front of him very carefully. Spotting a place where a section of the cliff edge was beginning to break free from the main body of cloud Ressa grabbed his hand and, finding the right moment, they jumped aboard a small, feathery cushion just as it pulled away from the shore.

Though the movement was gentle and steady, Zeeglit sat slap bang in the middle of his small island as it set off.

'Come away from the edge,' he said to Ressa who was looking around for other cloudlets they might collide with, although even he tried to avoid looking over the edge and down into the depths below.

This area was quite busy with ships of white sailing across the wide expanse of blue and they could see a few other moogles riding their craft, though they were too far off to speak to. Then, up ahead, Ressa saw a slightly larger pillow of floss drifting towards them and he knew they should jump across. However, when he tried to get Zeeglit to stand with him, he found him frozen to the spot, the fear of taking a leap and missing utmost in his mind. As the pillow drifted past, Ressa felt rather frustrated and he was determined to go for it when the next opportunity arose. He didn't have long to wait and this time he had Zeeglit on his feet in plenty of time and they made ready to jump.

As their tiny island gently nudged the other, Ressa shouted, 'Jump!' and Zeeglit plucked up his courage and jumped with his father, landing safely on the larger body of floss. Once again, he moved into the centre and sat down. It was a little longer this time before his path crossed with another cloudlet but once again, they made ready and jumped safely. As he looked back, he realised he had come more than half way across the void.

Still Zeeglit did not feel relaxed and he felt sure he would never become accustomed to this form of transport: there was too much time to think about what lay below and the consequences of an unsteady landing! It was necessary to travel on five more stages before they finally reached the far shore and were able to jump onto a very welcome expanse of solid white floss.

Walking a safe distance from the edge, Zeeglit sat down for a few moments to recover whilst Ressa searched around for an established path heading in the right direction. Using his dimometer to check he was on track, Ressa called to Zeeglit and they strode firmly away from the jumping stones and on toward the station at Pobble.

It was late morning when they came around a bend and saw the bright colours of a rainbow up ahead. Now, to those of us who live on the earth, a rainbow is a magical sign that appears in the sky when there is both rain and sunshine at the same time. However, what most of us don't realise is that these special circumstances are caused by the laughter and tears that result from a moogle wedding.

Ressa quickened his pace and Zeeglit scampered excitedly alongside in the hope of seeing the festivities as a moogle wedding is always a sight to behold. As they got closer, the sounds of celebration reached their ears and Ressa pointed out the happy couple at the heart of the event, standing under the centre of the colourful arc above.

The dress worn by the bride was of the finest gossamer lace which sparkled in the sunlight and moved gently in the warm breeze that played around her. Her partner was dressed in a tunic of grey with a gossamer collar that glistened with the same silvery threads. The many moogles who had gathered to help them celebrate their special occasion, wore their finest garments and happy smiles lit their faces.

As Zeeglit watched, the bride and groom; ceremony over, led the way along a path formed by ice crystals that had been laid through the floss towards the wedding feast, set out in all its splendour under the rainbow canopy.

Now moogles are very generous creatures indeed and once a young moogles spotted them watching the proceedings, Ressa and Zeeglit were quickly invited to take their place on a cushion of catilly straw and join in the festivities.

Ressa sat by a moogle of a similar age to himself who quickly introduced himself with the usual moogle greeting:

'Hi-lo and welcome friends. I am Raylee and this is my partner, Pagloo. Opposite are our three youngsters: Bim, Doon and Zig. Have you come far?'

Zeeglit felt the warmth of the welcome and listened as his father introduced himself and his son as platters of food and jugs of nip were passed around the table. Nip is the only mildly alcoholic drink available on the stratus and it is only drunk in small measures at times of celebration, stress or medical need. Served in a dish made from ice, it is best drunk as cold as possible – just before it freezes – and it is a deep brown colour, being made from the crushed grain of the compty grass. This particular crop grows in the areas nearest to the equator where it is harvested when ripe, stripped and trodden underfoot to extract the juice which is then stored for many months before it is ready to drink.

During the feast, which consisted of several courses and food of various forms and flavours, Ressa explained where they had come from and why they were travelling whilst Zeeglit chatted to Zig who was a similar age to him and seated opposite.

'We are not aware of this problem on the Alto but then, as the middle of the cloud layers, we are often protected from conditions above and below the other zones. What you describe sounds extremely worrying but I may be able to help you.' And with that, he passed along a platter of berries in the most beautiful shade of pale pink.

Ressa and Zeeglit had never seen their like before and they carefully took a small handful. It was a taste even Ressa didn't recognise but which was particularly delicious: sweet and slightly scented, leaving a subtle flavour on the tongue.

Raylee went on to explain: 'This is the mimberry: a tiny fruit which grows in a valley two days journey to the north. A small drop of the berry's juice goes a long way and the sweetness may help to disguise the sour flavour of the tuft in your homeland. As it happens, my sons and I are due to set off in the morning to gather berries to stock our larder for the winter. You would be more than welcome to join us.'

As he savoured the flavour, Ressa wondered if a short detour from their path would be worthwhile if he could take home a small handful of these special berries for Augil.

Hesitating briefly, Ressa turned to his son. 'I suppose it wouldn't be much of a delay in our journey for such a tempting prize. What do you think, Zeeglit?'

Still munching on a few of the berries, Zeeglit nodded enthusiastically and the matter was settled.

'Come,' encouraged Raylee, his voice resonating with a warm welcome. 'Stay with us tonight and we'll leave at first light. There is a moonbeam port not too far from the mimberry valley so you won't have to retrace your steps.'

It was soon agreed that the travellers would spend the night with the family then join them on their mission.

Raylee's family burrow was only a short walk from the wedding celebrations and the moon lit the way as they strolled home with the family at the end of a very happy day. As a cluster of burrows came into view, Zig scampered ahead to take in the glow lamps.

As Zeeglit ducked his head to enter the burrow, he noticed that this home glowed with the rays of orange lamps mirroring the warmth he felt from their new friends. Pagloo and Raylee bustled about making sure there would be a comfortable nest for their overnight guest whilst Zeeglit took a look around their home.

A short entrance tunnel ended in a circular chamber with several pods leading off to the sides. The boys took Zeeglit into one of these; cluttered with their surf-boards and other bits and pieces, and bathed in a purple glow from their lamp. They chatted about all sorts of things as Ressa wandered into the kitchen area with yellow glow-worms in the lantern hanging in its centre. It was neat and orderly with a row of platters, propped on a cabinet against an outer wall, reflected flashes of yellow light as Ressa moved around the chamber. There was the familiar smell of burning hydrogen gas, extracted from the air and used to heat all moogle burrows, and the fire-box crackled comfortingly away in the corner.

The central chamber was on two levels: a walkway around the outside with a sunken area in the centre where the family relaxed against pillows of floss to chatter about the day and play games which were housed in a transparent trunk at one side.

As they needed to make an early start the next day, the family decided to settle down for the night. Zeeglit lay awake for only a short while, thinking over all they had seen and done in a short time and their good fortune in meeting such friendly creatures, before he drifted off into an undisturbed night's sleep.

Chapter 4
A Close Encounter

As they set out the following morning, Zeeglit thought the sky was a rather eerie shade of grey and an unexplained shiver ran down his back.

Shrugging it off as nonsense, he gathered his pack and keeping close to Ressa, they set off in a new direction with Raylee and his sons: Bim, Doom and Zig, three strapping young moogles, each carrying a pack in which to bring home their fruit.

During the day, they walked, rested and walked some more, making good progress yet Zeeglit couldn't shake off the feeling that something wasn't quite right but when he mentioned it to his father, he told him everything was fine.

As the afternoon wore on and the sun dipped lower towards the horizon, the ground over which they walked became more uneven and their journey became slower. It was hard work clambering over raised areas and taking care to avoid sudden dips.

Gradually, the remaining rays of the sun were hidden from view as a large overhanging mass of dull grey vapour drifted above them. The air became saturated with a fine, penetrating mist which seeped into their fur, making it heavy, and Zeeglit began to feel rather cold.

With the disappearing sunlight, nightfall came quickly and they decided to make camp and hope that the conditions would improve by morning.

'What about here?' Raylee suggested, indicating a semi-circular area of smooth, grey scree, backed by a deeper bank which looked like a suitable place to scoop out a burrow for their night's shelter.

This rather wild, grey uninhabited area seemed to have cast a strange atmosphere over the small group making their night's shelter and Zeeglit realised the others had also begun to feel rather uneasy. They found themselves talking in hushed whispers and looking over their shoulders as they took turns to dig.

The younger moogles took the first shifts at digging: their youthful energy making up for their smaller paws, but Ressa and Raylee also took their turn.

As Zeeglit scooped the scree behind him, he marvelled – not for the first time – how the consistency of the clouds surface varied in different places. Here, it was sharp and gritty; areas of compacted ice making it necessary to include twists and turns in the burrow which, in turn, made it take longer to dig.

Taking a break to rub his thick leathery paws, now sore from the rough material he'd been working with, Zeeglit made way for Doon to continue the job. Looking warily around, he gave a shudder and thought he'd be glad when they could get safely tucked away from this hostile environment.

Discarded scree, passed back along the tunnel, was mounded up outside the entrance to disguise its whereabouts and finally, feeling cold, bedraggled and more than a little scared, the group covered their tracks and made their way into the hastily dug sleeping chamber. They decided that they would take it in turns to keep watch at the entrance and Zig volunteered to take the first shift. Curled up together for warmth, and exhausted from their digging, it didn't take any of them long to fall asleep.

Zeeglit was awoken at first light by Doon shaking his arm and indicating the need for silence. Creeping along to the entrance with the others, he saw with horror a group of half a dozen thordite males passing a hundred metres away.

The thordites live in the deepest, darkest of all the clouds and rarely cross paths with moogles: indeed, Zeeglit had wondered if they really existed as he'd never met anyone who had actually seen one.

Now, he felt the hairs on the back of his neck stand on end and all those in the burrow held their breath in terror as those dreaded creatures strode by.

Unlike moogles, the fur of a thordite looks greasy and uncared for. They walk with slightly stooped backs but still stand at least twice as tall as an average moogle. This group were unaware of the moogles hiding so close by and this gave the friends a good chance to study them. With pinched, angular faces they walked in twos and threes and chatted in a relaxed manner though Zeeglit noticed all of them carried a graplar: their fabled weapon of attack. These weapons were crude but very effective. Thick twine wound around the long handle of the weapon, finishing in a loop which the thordite would keep around their wrist in times of conflict. A quick stinging blow could be delivered by flicking the gantate at an enemy or, for a more intense attack, the warrior would grip the handle and use the highly polished club end (carved from rock-hard black Bru-glit roots) to beat their foes.

They wore tunics made from a tough-looking fabric that Zeeglit didn't recognise but the dark grey of the cloth added to their general drab appearance.

A few moments later, the group had disappeared round a mound and it was agreed in quick whispers, that Bim: Raylee's eldest, should follow at a distance to make sure they had left the area before the group left the shelter of their burrow.

After a strained half hour, Bim slipped quietly back down the passageway.

He reported that he had followed the small group of thordites for a while when they were joined by a larger group moving in the same direction. Talking excitedly, they disappeared over a ridge.

'I dropped to the floor and crawled to the edge and looked over. Gathered below me, about fifty thordites were clustered in groups; relaxing, eating and looking in no hurry to move on.'

'Could you hear anything they said?' asked Zig.

'No,' Bim replied. 'Their chatter was quick and their voices hard to make out.'

'I suggest we cover the entrance to the burrow and sit tight for the day then leave under the cover of darkness,' said Raylee and they all agreed.

Whilst Ressa was disappointed to delay his journey once again, he had to agree that it was a sensible suggestion – the thought of meeting a group of thordites face-to-face was horrifying as no one knew what might happen.

After using the unexpected break to catch up on some sleep, Raylee and his sons carefully cleared the entrance to their hiding place.

A murky darkness had crept into the clearing and, using its cover, the small group crept out and tiptoed quietly on their way, carefully skirting around the area Bim identified as the thordites camp. It wasn't until they had covered quite some distance and the moon was high in the sky that the friends felt slightly more confident that they'd left danger behind.

They talked in hushed tones about the thordites and why they might be in the area. Raylee was positive they'd never been seen in that region before. He had heard that large groups occasionally moved to a new home-site, keeping to back-routes and avoiding confrontation.

They all hoped this was the case now but Raylee decided they would need to check up on the clan on their return journey to make sure they were no longer in the area.

As darkness finally slid over the horizon, they entered a wide valley and thoughts of recent experiences fled from their minds. The scenery changed, the sky lightened and moogles could be seen in all directions: moving amongst the floss, gathering mimberries.

Zig and Doon raced ahead to find a likely spot to dig as Bim explained that the berries are found just under the surface. When they are ripe, they give a tell-tale red glow, seen from the Oodle Pool as a red sky at sunrise or sunset.

As Zeeglit joined Zig, Doon was already on all fours, carefully moving the top layers of floss aside to reveal a cluster of glossy red berries.

The group quickly settled where the red glow indicated a good harvest beneath. Zeeglit took his, now empty, nimbo-tuft canister from his pack and knelt down. Gently, he moved the floss and gazed on a rash of beautiful red berries. He stretched out his hand and, as he plucked his first mimberry from its vine, a beautiful scent filled the air.

So rich was the crop, berries quickly followed one another into his container and by late morning Zeeglit's container was full. He lay on his back, nestled in the soft pillows of floss cast aside during his morning's work, and closed his eyes. The air was heavy with the rich, heady aroma of mimberries and he could hear Ressa and Raylee chatting as they continued to work.

He must have dozed off because the excited chatter of a family of moogles passing close by reached his ears, reminding Zeeglit of his family at home. A stab of homesickness caused him to wonder if they were all missing him as much as he was them and for the first time, he felt guilty about leaving home without telling his mother. However, he didn't have long to worry as Ressa called across.

'Ready, Sleepyhead? I think it's time we made our way.'

Reluctantly, he dragged himself to his feet and after a fond farewell to Raylee and his sons, the travellers headed back out of the valley and turned in the opposite direction to last night's burrow, towards a moonbeam port a short distance away.

At midday they sat down to take a short rest and Ressa referred to his dimometer to make sure they were heading in the right direction. However, they'd not been sat for long when they heard a strange whimpering sound coming from a little way off the track. The sound was unlike anything Zeeglit had heard before and he was unsure what to do.

'Shh!' motioned Ressa, who was on high alert.

After listening for a little longer, he decided it sounded as if something was in trouble. 'Stay here. I'll see what it is,' Ressa whispered and being a kindly soul, he gathered his courage and crept towards the eerie sound. He became further alarmed as he edged his way across a dangerously dark area of floss and suddenly spotted the source of the sound.

Lying in an awkward position with its leg resting at a strange angle lay a young thordite, shivering and moaning in obvious pain. Conflicting emotions of sympathy and horror chased through his brain as the creature's suffering reached out to Ressa whilst the whereabouts of its clan and the dark floss were a cause of great concern.

One particularly heartfelt cry, however, brought Ressa to the youngster's side and, as he dropped to his knees, he also saw fear in the eyes of the young thordite. Softly, whispering words of reassurance, Ressa swiftly adjusted the youngster's position and carefully felt along the leg. He felt sure it was broken in a couple of places.

With his ability to heal bones and other injuries as well as illnesses, Ressa was one of the few moogles who would be able to help. Quickly, he held his palms against the position of the breaks to allow the healing warmth to creep into the leg and mend the bones.

Slowly, the whimpering ceased and the fear in the thordite's eyes was replaced by wonder as it realised it was no longer in pain. Ressa sat down and wondered what to do next when his companion began to speak in a strange nasal tone which made it difficult to understand but he was able to make out that she was called Lexron. She had wandered off from the clan two days earlier and, in her panic, had lost her sense of direction, wandering onto the dark floss the previous night without realising it was there.

The dark floss is extremely dangerous as it is the storage area for the natural electricity known to us as lightening, released by thordites in their displays of strength and power, but extremely unstable and not somewhere to take a stroll.

As Lexron had crossed the dark floss, a bright flash from the storage area had terrified her and she'd swerved to avoid it, twisting her leg awkwardly and being brought down by the pain.

Ressa realised what a delicate position they were both in and carefully, together, they began to edge back across the darkness towards Zeeglit. Suddenly, the dark floss began to shake and forks of lightening flashed around them!

Grabbing Lexron and pulling her along with him, Ressa steered a careful path between the flashes to the safety of the lighter floss where Zeeglit was on his feet looking very worried. They flopped down, breathing hard and laughing with relief as Ressa quickly explained the situation to his son.

Ressa's laughter was short-lived though for, as he sat up, he saw a sight which turned his blood cold: alerted by the firework action, a group of thordite warriors were making their way rapidly towards them! Sunlight glanced off the tips of their graplars and this group looked far more alert than his previous sighting.

To stand and run would be fruitless as the longer legs of the thordites would quickly overtake them; particularly weighed down as Ressa was under his heavy pack.

As the Thordites drew close, his companion jumped to her feet waving her arms, and ran towards them. She threw herself at the apparent leader of the clan who gathered her in his arms and the two jabbered rapidly together as the rest of the warriors stood around the moogles in a very intimidating manner and Zeeglit again huddled close to his father feeling more terrified than ever before.

Up close, the warrior's fur could be seen to be tangled and greasy and gave off a generally unpleasant, sour smell. Zeeglit tried not to wrinkle his nose and decided it was better to avoid eye contact with these unfriendly creatures. After what felt like an eternity, the circle of guards parted and the thordite leader, with Lexron by his side, stood over him. A trembling Ressa pulled Zeeglit to his feet and waited to hear their fate.

The leader, who introduced himself as Blauron, began to speak in a strange deep voice with the same nasal tones as Lexron.

'It appears that I have you to thank for saving my daughter. I had heard of the healing powers possessed by moogles but never thought to see it practiced on a member of my clan. She is a foolish youngster who has now seen the error of her ways.

Had you not come along and had the courage and compassion to cross the dark floss, this story could have had a very different ending. We will be forever in your debt and I wish you every blessing on your way.'

With that, the clan turned to follow their leader, leaving two speechless moogles to once again flop down onto the floss to get their breath back.

Chapter 5
Ice-Cirrus for Tea

Realising that they could still reach the transit zone in time for the night's moonbeams, Ressa and Zeeglit gathered their belongings and set off at a brisk walk. They had plenty to talk about and it didn't seem long before they reached the entrance to the port.

The area was very busy with many moogles heading down to the Nimbo-Stratus but Ressa was not yet ready to return home. His ultimate goal was still to harvest the ice-cirrus and it was with this in mind that he put aside his fear and pulled Zeeglit into a strong shaft for their upward journey.

It was a clear, bright night and the stars twinkled from beyond the shaft. This time, the passage was smooth but the distance was long and Zeeglit was tired when he finally arrived at the port on the Cirro-Stratus.

As he stepped from the beam, he immediately noticed a sharp drop in temperature and the thinner air made him catch his breath. The bright moonbeams of the portal area gave him a clear view of the moogles scurrying around and Zeeglit was struck by how few there were compared to the ports on the lower levels. Ressa explained that they would sleep close by for the rest of the hours of darkness then ask around for information about the fields of ice-cirrus.

There didn't seem to be any sign of a stay-by so, once they'd found a likely site, Ressa began to dig a burrow. Zeeglit offered to help and was given the job of banking up the scree to give some extra protection from the cold wind that had sprung up. This time, Ressa dug deeper than usual to reach some extra warmth as the icy atmosphere nipped at his bones. Finally, huddled together deep inside, they fell asleep, wondering what tomorrow would reveal.

When he woke the following morning, Zeeglit was colder than he'd ever been before. Quickly, he pulled his spare waistcoat on for extra warmth then, anxious to show no weakness; he made his way out of the burrow and shivered as he stood in the bright, chill morning air.

The view before him was stunning and Zeeglit stood blinking in the bright light as he took in what he could see: bright blue above and way below, through a gap in the floss, the Oodle Pool glistened like a rare jewel with various shades of blue and green. The floss around him was fine and pure white, with strands of silver sparkling in the sunlight but rather too cold for a morning roll in the dew and Ressa agreed he would do as he was for once!

Unsure of which way to head, Zeeglit suggested they retraced their steps the short distance to the port they had arrived at the previous night. Here, they managed to find an old-timer who assured them that the best fields of ice-cirrus were to be found half a day's trek to the east.

'Mind you,' he warned, 'Beware of the shifting floss at this high level. You will also find your journey much slower than on lower levels due to the thinner atmosphere.'

At this point, I must introduce a brief geography lesson, by explaining that clouds are formed in three layers, named in the ancient language of Latin.

At the lowest of these layers, Nimbostratus can be found. These clouds are formed mainly of water vapour. Mid-level clouds are also composed mainly of water droplets but some ice crystals do appear and it is at this level that you find the Altostratus. Climbing higher still, you reach the Cirrostratus where the temperatures are so cold, the clouds are formed primarily of ice crystals, giving a wispy, white appearance.

It is on the middle and lower layers that most moogle activity takes place as the thin, unstable layer of the Cirrostratus makes it a very dangerous place to be.

The floss is much finer and more brittle than lower levels and travellers sometimes find themselves in trouble as the area they are walking across will suddenly shift, become wispy then disappear, making it extremely dangerous and one of the main reasons few moogles travel this high.

'Thank you. We'll be careful,' replied Zeeglit as he turned to move off.

Sure enough, the travellers found the need to stop and rest several times during the morning to catch their breath and enjoy this unusual landscape. However, at noon they came over the brow of a hill of floss and gasped with delight at the sight that met their eyes.

Scattered over the plain before them were silver plants coated with tufts of iridescent, glistening ice-cirrus. Zeeglit stood for several minutes just gazing at the scene before following his father who was striding towards the shrubs.

Suddenly, with no warning at all, Zeeglit was aware of a change in the floss around him and a couple of metres ahead, a gap appeared. Terrified, he watched it extend to left and right and all around him holes began to appear, revealing a terrifying drop! Zeeglit stood perfectly still, too frightened to shout out, watching the shifting pattern around him, hoping desperately that the floss he was standing on would remain.

At this point, Ressa turned around to see where he was. Horrified but unable to help, he shouted out.

'Stand still. Look for a chance to jump!'

However, the holes continued to widen and Zeeglit thought he would find himself standing on fresh air when, suddenly, he noticed another section of floss had broken away from the mass and was drifting towards him.

'Over there!' shouted Ressa.

'I know; I'm watching it,' replied Zeeglit and willing it to come his way, Zeeglit held his breath and waited.

Slowly, slowly, the cloud mass drifted nearer and, just when he thought he would surely fall, it came within jumping distance. Zeeglit leapt with all his strength, landing safely on the drifting floss, just in time to look back and see the last remaining wisps fade away. Fortunately, his drifting platform made its way towards the area of bushes he'd seen earlier and nestled securely into the main body of floss.

Realising how lucky he was to be alive made Zeeglit wonder if he'd been foolish to come all this way. Ressa rushed across and gathered him in a hug, regretting his decision to let his son travel with him and he felt very worried about the rest of his time on the Cirrostratus.

Gingerly, both moogles stepped ahead, frightened now of where to put each footfall. Carefully, slowly, they made their way towards the nearest shrub.

Cautiously Zeeglit reached out and touched the nearest cluster of sparkling strands which felt feather-soft and slightly sticky to his touch. He gave a gentle tug and several strands came away from their silvery branch.

As if in slow motion, Zeeglit raised them to his mouth and popped them in. His eyes widened with surprise as the delicacy fizzed on his tongue; giving off the most delicious flavour you could ever imagine!

'Well?' asked Ressa who had done the same.

'Wow!' was the response and Ressa and Zeeglit spent many minutes feasting on more than was good for them. Finally, Ressa removed his collecting net from his pack and set about his business. Zeeglit did the same but as they worked carefully, so as not to damage the delicate tufts, they constantly kept one eye on the ground around them.

Plucking handfuls from each branch and dropping them into the net, they moved from shrub to shrub. Each cluster weighed little but it was surprising how quickly the net became heavy as Zeeglit moved from bush to bush and before too long Zeeglit realised he could carry no more.

He was thrilled to think of arriving home with his new-found treasure but desperate to leave this dangerous environment, he was pleased when Ressa announced they would try and make it back to the port and catch a shaft all the way to the lower level before resting.

However, it was not to be. They hadn't gone far along the path before a party of five locals came the other way; recognisable by their very distinctive pale grey and white fur.

'Hi-lo and welcome friends,' came the familiar greeting. A middle-aged male seemed to be travelling with his family and they stopped to talk. 'You are obviously not from these parts. Have you come for the show?'

'Hi-lo, friend. We're not lost but I am worried about the shifting floss – We had a near miss earlier and I'm keen to get back to the moonbeam port. What show?'

'Oh, you can't leave without seeing the show! This is the night when the stars fly – it only happens like this once in a blue moon (hence the familiar saying here on Earth!). You must come with us and see it – we'll keep you safe. You won't be sorry.'

'I know it's late,' added his partner, 'but you can come back and stay with us after and leave tomorrow. You really would miss a treat.'

Without a clue as to what he was about to see, Ressa felt this was too good an opportunity to miss.

'What do you think?' he asked Zeeglit.

Dangers forgotten at the thought of an adventure, Zeeglit said he thought they should stay for one more night and so turned to walk back the way they had just come with the family. A group of five youngsters danced around their parents in obvious excitement as they walked along and introductions were made.

Donment and his partner, Lismis, explained that the conditions were just right to see a fantastic display of shooting stars. Whilst they can be seen occasionally from the lower cloud layers, the clarity of the air at this high level and the lack of any further clouds above mean that there is an uninterrupted view. Once a year there is a particularly spectacular display and this was such a night. As they headed towards a well-known viewing area, more and more moogles could be seen, hurrying along paths from all directions.

Zeeglit was still very anxious about the ground beneath his feet and Donment saw him casting wary glances around him.

'Don't worry,' he said. 'You get to know where the difficult areas are for walking and there is never a problem in this region. The floss here is thick and stable.'

Breathing a sigh of relief, Zeeglit relaxed and was soon playing around with the other young moogles. As they joined a great crowd of others on a high plateau, Ressa felt quite reassured: surely so many locals would not bring their youngsters to an area where they might be in danger and he decided to forget about his earlier experience for now and see what all the fuss was about.

By now, the sun had dipped below the horizon and there was a definite chill in the air. The sky was a deep shade of navy and millions of stars twinkled above. Zeeglit watched as the mottled globe of the moon crept higher and higher into the night sky; seeming particularly huge tonight as he was closer to it than ever before.

As they waited, Ressa chatted to Donment and Lismis and told them of his reason for travelling to this level. They were very worried when he told them about the food problems at home and hoped that his family would enjoy the treats he was bringing them. They shared stories about their youngsters and Zeeglit told his new friends about his family at home who seemed particularly far away tonight.

All around them, intergenerational clusters of moogles chatted and laughed. Some stood, others sat; some had brought food and flasks of nip could be seen being handed around groups of adults – it was certainly cold enough for it! Youngsters frolicked and chased each other and old friends greeted each other with great enthusiasm. The carnival atmosphere was contagious and Zeeglit found he was enjoying himself when, all of a sudden, a gasp of awe silenced the crowd and all eyes turned towards the sky.

For a moment Zeeglit saw nothing, then a single brilliant bead of pure white light, followed by a tapering tail of fading brilliance, drew a line across the midnight blue velvet of the sky and disappeared. A few seconds later, another sudden blaze of white flashed across in front of him and the show had begun.

Thick and fast, the little white lines came streaking out of the heavens and it was difficult to know which way to look for the best. Zeeglit was just thinking how glad he was that he hadn't missed the spectacle, when things got even more impressive: a particularly heavy shower of stars flashed past and he was overawed to see the surface of the moon glow blue with their reflected light!

The crowd shouted and cheered at the incredible sight and Zeeglit knew it was a moment he would always treasure. Slowly, the display faded and families began to drift away home.

'Well?' asked Lismis, simply.

'Thank you so much,' Ressa replied. 'I had no idea! What did you think, Zeeglit?'

'It was wonderful. I'll never forget it!'

'Ah well, that's that for another year. That sight always thrills me and I can't help wondering how far some of those stars have come,' said Donment. 'Home time,' he called to the youngsters and the group moved off down the path. It was almost dawn by the time they reached the family burrow and Zeeglit was curled up snug and warm in their central chamber before he realised he hadn't given another thought to the shifting floss.

When he awoke and opened his eyes the following morning, Zeeglit struggled to think for a moment where he was. He could see that the roof above his head was smooth but it was quite dark in the burrow and he couldn't recognise his surroundings. The sound of young moogles playing was coming from a pod close by and he remembered the events of the night before and the kind family who had invited them back to stay.

Thinking it must be very early as it was still quite dark, he was just about to turn over and try to get back to sleep when Lismis came bustling through.

'Oh, I hope I didn't wake you,' she said.

'No, not at all. Couldn't you sleep?' asked Zeeglit.

Lismis laughed. 'I slept too well after last night's excitement. The sun is high in the sky and half the day has passed already. Your father is outside and ready for the day.'

'I had no idea,' said Zeeglit, sitting up. 'Of course, your burrow is extra deep because of the cold. I'm not used to the darkness!'

Getting up, he followed Lismis outside and blinked in the bright sunlight. Ressa and Donment were sitting close by, playing with one of the young and they turned to greet Zeeglit.

'Hi-lo, friend,' said Donment. 'I hope you slept well. You were sound asleep when Flin and I crept through earlier. He finds it difficult to sleep much beyond dawn whatever has gone on the day before!'

'I don't think I would have woken if you'd walked right over me,' Zeeglit responded. 'I think this high altitude is making me more tired than usual.'

Thinking that he had better spend some time on his personal hygiene as he'd missed out the day before, he excused himself and spent a little while grooming his fur. Although he still found it very cold, it did not seem as bad as the previous morning and he was able to enjoy looking around this foreign landscape.

From where he was sitting, Zeeglit could see that the high ground where they had been to watch the spectacular show the night before, stretched in a great arc behind them like the sides of a huge dish, sloping down to a lower area in front. Looking towards the horizon in the distance, he gazed over endless folds of snow-white floss capped by a rich blue ceiling and he thought what a beautiful morning it was. Light glanced off something that sparkled in the middle distance and he wondered if it was the bushes of ice cirrus that he had visited the day before but he couldn't be sure as he had quite lost his bearings with the detour they had made during the night.

There seemed to be the entrances to a large number of burrows quite close together and when he mentioned this to his host, he explained that they deliberately create a warren of burrows with their chambers close together, deep under the surface, so any warmth they can create is shared around: a type of basic central heating. Each family has their hydrogen gas fire to heat their own burrow at night and this heat radiates through the ground for a short distance, ensuring the whole warren maintains some warmth through the daylight hours.

Zeeglit was very impressed with this system and the cooperation between families. Many moogles of varying ages were going about their daily business and several stopped for a word on their way past. One of these was a young female who was introduced as Snippit and when she heard that Ressa and Zeeglit were to travel back to a lower level that day she said that she too was travelling to the moonbeam port later that afternoon and would be happy to show them the way.

The journey across the delicate floss had been troubling Ressa somewhat: although he wasn't a nervous moogle, the thought that the ground could just disappear under your feet was not good and he realised you needed a certain local knowledge to walk far on this level. With that worry taken care of, he was able to relax and enjoy the next few hours chatting and dozing under the warmth of the afternoon sun.

Zeeglit was once again able to enjoy cloud surfing with the other youngsters and he was impressed to see the speeds reached by some of the others. When he mentioned this, he was told that it was because the surface was particularly icy when compacted.

It was as the sun dipped over the hills behind the burrows that they said goodbye to their new friends. Thanking them for showing them the wonderful display and making them so welcome, they set off towards the port with Snippit. With her youth and being used to the thinner air, she set off at quite a pace, and Ressa had to ask her to slow down a bit as he was puffing and panting as he struggled to keep up.

Their route was straightforward, with solid ground under their feet all the way, though Zeeglit still found it strange to have no ceiling of clouds above his head and he realised it made him feel quite insecure.

Unfortunately, the night was overcast and when they reached the port, they found that the moonbeams were short.

Ressa realised they would need to break their homeward journey for an extra night and he decided to pay a return visit to Raylee to check they had returned home safely and to hear if they had any news of the thordites.

Thanking Snippit for her help, he selected a suitable moonbeam and together Ressa and Zeeglit stepped into the centre of the shaft. It was rather a dull journey as the sky was too hazy to see anything but it gave both moogles a chance to reflect on all they had seen on the Cirrostratus. Whilst he was glad to have been, it was not something Zeeglit thought he would ever do again. He would certainly advise his own youngsters against journeying that high in the future: even the thought of trying to cross the shifting floss made him shudder and he could only wonder how his own father must have felt – standing so close but unable to do anything to help.

Chapter 6
Bad News

After grabbing a few hours rest at a stay-by near the port, Ressa whistled a rambling tune as Zeeglit surfed alongside as they made their way towards their friend's home next morning. However, when they got there, Ressa's first thought was that the family were out as there were no signs of life. Although disappointed, he decided to make doubly sure and shouted a cheery greeting.

'Hi-lo. Anyone home?'

There was no friendly reply and Ressa was just wondering what to do when Pagloo appeared in the entrance to the burrow: shoulders stooped and eyes troubled.

'Hi-lo, and sorry to keep you waiting,' she began. 'Things have not been good since we last saw you. Come along in; Raylee will be pleased to see you and he'll explain everything.'

Greatly troubled, Ressa motioned to Zeeglit and they followed her down the passageway and into the central chamber. Raylee lay curled up in a nest of catilly grass with his head resting on one arm.

Dropping down beside him, Ressa was horrified to see how unwell his friend looked: his fur was limp and lack-lustre and his eyes, dull.

'What has happened? Are you ill?' Ressa enquired.

'Ah friend, it is worse than you can ever imagine!' And Raylee began his tale.

'After we parted company, we finished harvesting berries then made our way carefully back to the clearing where the thordite camp had been. All that remained were trampled areas of floss and tracks that lead away to the south-east. We then followed the tracks for half a day before deciding the clan were definitely moving away before turning back and heading for home.'

He did not need to add that they had all been secretly relieved not to have found anything more than traces of the thordites!

'Then, two nights ago, our sleep was broken in the early hours by intruders in the burrow. Before we knew what was happening, a warrior troop of thordites had bound Bim and Doon and I was just in time to see them being dragged from their pod as I came out of ours. I rushed forward but my way was blocked by three burly, aggressive warriors. They beat me to the floor and attacked me with their graplars as I lay helpless.'

At that moment, Zig appeared from the passageway and expressed his pleasure at seeing Ressa and Zeeglit. He explained that he had been away overnight visiting a friend when the incident had occurred, thereby avoiding the warriors. He had just been out to see if there was any way of tracking their attackers.

Horrified, Ressa asked about the extent of his friend's injuries and Zeeglit sat quietly in a corner taking it all in. Once again blessing his given power, Ressa set about healing the many breaks and bruises. This helped Raylee feel more comfortable but his beating had been so severe, it would be a while before he was active.

Pagloo cried with relief at the effect on her partner and then bustled off to prepare food to tempt the invalid and reward the guests whilst the males discussed what could be done.

Raylee was anxious to know what Zig had discovered and, once he was sure his father was resting as comfortably as possible, he revealed that he had found thordite tracks leading off to the north and, upon questioning locals from nearby burrows, it appeared that several other families had suffered the same fate: eleven moogle youths having been taken in total, with no strong adults left behind to retaliate.

After a quick bite to eat, Ressa's healing powers were put to good use as he helped to heal other moogles who had been attacked and it was midnight before he was able to sit down with the others to discuss what to do. He was very concerned about Raylee and wanted to stay and keep an eye on him whilst Zig said he needed to follow the thordite tracks to try and find his brothers. Zeeglit wanted to go too but naturally his father was against this and arguments continued into the night. However, Zig did seem a very responsible character and eventually it was decided that, after a few hours' sleep, Zeeglit and Zig would leave at dawn in an attempt to do all they could to return the captives to their homes.

So, as the first fingers of sunlight crept across the floss, Zeeglit promised his father that he wouldn't do anything dangerous and, armed with only Ressa's dimometer and gantate (fog lamp) and Zig's company, he set off into the unknown.

Once they had picked up the trail, it was easy enough to follow. It was obvious there had been a large gathering of thordites and a clear path had been carved through the floss – its creators apparently unconcerned about being followed as they had left no able-bodied adults to worry about.

Zeeglit and Zig made swift progress and talked only rarely to conserve their energy. They had been walking steadily for a few hours when Zig laid a paw on Zeeglit's arm and they stood still.

Zig's young ears had picked up a hum coming from their left. Quietly, they changed direction and left the main track to see what was making the mournful sound: Zeeglit keeping an eye on his dimometer to ensure they would be able to find their way back.

The sound became louder as they moved forward and could only be described as a low moaning: a sound so full of despair it made your spirits sink and Zeeglit dreaded what they were going to find.

However, when they did come over the top of a hill of floss and see the origin of the sound, they didn't initially know what to make of it: sat around in a large circle, five of the strangest creatures Zeeglit had ever seen were hunched over; facing inwards and moaning. A quick intake of breath from Zig and,

'I don't believe it – they don't exist!' caused Zeeglit to ask in a whisper, 'What are they?'

'I think,' Zig replied, 'though I can't be sure, that they are Glums. These mythological creatures appear in tales passed down through the generations but no one has ever seen one and it is generally assumed that they don't exist.'

'What are they?' asked Zeeglit, again, keeping a wary eye on the strange moaning creatures.

'They are ancient creatures that are reported to appear when there are times of great tragedy and they meet at the site of a catastrophe.'

'But there doesn't seem to be any great problem here,' commented Zeeglit, surveying the scene before them.

The five creatures, each about four times the height and general build of a moogle, were sat on the floss, knees drawn up and shoulders rounded, with their heads, draped in wild silver tresses, bent forward so their faces could not be seen.

'Look at the floss,' Zig ordered suddenly. Dragging his attention from the strange creatures, Zeeglit began to notice that the area of floss between the Glums was, indeed, different. It looked charred and, on closer inspection, appeared to be throbbing.

'Wait here!' ordered Zig as he made to creep forward.

'No way!' replied Zeeglit and nodding in agreement Zig motioned him to be quiet.

Together, the two moogles crept closer, wary of the reception they would receive. However, they needn't have worried as the as the Glums kept their heads down and continued to give out their low, heart-rending moans.

Between the tragic figures, the floss was indeed singed and darker than the surrounding area. The surface throbbed rhythmically like a gentle heartbeat and the moogles were mystified to know what was happening.

Approaching the nearest creature, Zig said cautiously, 'Hi-lo, stranger. What is happening here?'

At first he thought he would receive no answer but then slowly, very slowly, the Glum turned towards them and Zeeglit found himself looking into a face that carried a whole world of worries. The large, round face with silvery-green skin stretched taught and almost translucent, was surrounded by a silvery halo of fine, wild hair, contained eyes that you felt you could drown in. Big brown pupils that swam in deep green pools of unshed tears held the worries of the entire world and its mouth, which was drawn into a moaning circle, closed for a moment as it looked at Zig.

Feeling inexplicably sad, Zig took a steadying breath and repeated his question. 'What has happened here?'

'Oh woe … (sigh) … Great troubles … (sigh) … Alas … (sigh) … The heavens have fallen … Oh woe!' came the deep resonating answer and the moaning resumed as, very slowly, his head turned back and lowered once again to his knees.

'What do you mean?' enquired Zig. 'Excuse me …' But there was no further response from the Glum.

'What now?' asked Zeeglit, whose nerves were inclined to make him giggle. 'Should we go?'

'No,' said Zig. 'These creatures haven't been seen for decades. They must be here for something serious. Let's think for a moment.'

Zeeglit dropped to his knees and inched his way slowly onto the charred floss. He could feel rhythmic vibrations from below and slowly, carefully, he began to pull the floss aside with his wide, sensitive paws. It wasn't long before he revealed a cavernous area and there, lying at the centre, Zeeglit could see the root of all the troubles: there, looking lost and forlorn, was a small, dim star.

Zig had just joined him to look into the hole when suddenly everything fell into place! No wonder there was a problem with the shrubs growing in the Valley of Nimbo – the stars are responsible for giving the tuft its nutrients as they shine down upon it at night. If a star had fallen out of place – an event never before known – it was bound to have a devastating effect.

Excitedly, Zeeglit explained his thoughts to Zig who agreed and the two decided that there was nothing they could do at that time but they would give the matter thought as they resumed their journey.

Marking the spot on the dimometer, Zeeglit followed the bearing to take them back to the thordite path and, just before dipping over the ridge, he looked back to see the five hunched figures still moaning and marking the disaster zone.

Chapter 7
The Ice Tower

For a while, their progress was steady, with a clear path to follow and no signs of recent thordite activity. Zeeglit was lost in his own thoughts about the fallen star and how the matter could be resolved and Zig was focussed on finding his brothers whilst worrying about what might be happening to them. Yet, their journey was destined to be eventful.

As they came round a bend in the path, a wall of ice-white floss drifted across and came to rest in front of them. A great tower-like structure seemed to be embedded in the centre of the wall and Zig pointed out a wide, veiled doorway leading inside.

They waited for a short period of time for it to move on again but it was immobile and, whilst Zeeglit was very wary, the dimometer pointed to there being no way around the mass so they decided to see if they could make their way through the tower to the other side as they didn't have time to waste. Calling a greeting at the entrance and receiving no response, they cautiously made their way inside and what a sight met their eyes!

Glowing ice-white with reflected light, the tower was hollow inside with spiral pathways leading upward, crisscrossing as they went. Hanging from every possible surface were thin threads of white, shimmering with the gentle breeze that wafted through. Giving out a low whistle and speaking in hushed tones as if in some mystical presence, Zig suggested they follow the main upward spiral as there was no obvious route straight through. Zeeglit, who had never seen anything more beautiful in his life, was happy to agree.

As they followed its upward path, they couldn't help but brush past the thousands of strands that hung across their way – feather-light though slightly sticky, they tickled their faces and the moogles giggled as they followed the incline, wondering at the creation of this enchanted place. However, the path seemed to be leading nowhere but up.

'I think we should retrace our steps and try another route – we don't seem to be getting anywhere,' Zig suggested after a short while.

They turned, with Zeeglit in the lead, but almost immediately, the younger moogle squealed in pain, holding his cheek and they stopped in horror; their pathway now blocked by the tower's inhabitants: one of which had given Zeeglit a small but nasty bite.

Vibrations caused when the white tendrils were disturbed, were the signal for the creator of each thread to descend in a crystal droplet to the tip of its creation. The tiny, silvery mites waited there for their prey to return down the pathway – there being no-where else for them to go.

Thinking quickly about their dangerous situation and unsure of the severity of the bites they would surely receive if they went back down the path, Zig had no choice but to lead the way upward though the pair now tried to avoid as many of the threads as they could – all the amusement and beauty gone from the game.

Up and up they continued, until the top of the tower was in sight. Their pathway became steeper and slippery and both moogles were clearly very worried about the trap they had walked into.

'I have an idea,' said Zeeglit. 'If we could dig our way through the walls, maybe we could slide down the outside.'

'Well, it's certainly worth a try,' replied Zig. 'I don't fancy our return route otherwise!'

They found a likely spot and started to scoop out the floss. Encouraged by the draught that they began to feel, they doubled their efforts and had soon carved enough of a gap to crawl through.

Gingerly, they looked out at the huge drop below them.

'If we lean inward, I think we may cut a groove in the side of the tower and not fall off,' suggested Zeeglit.

Using Zeeglit's waistcoat as a mat, they carefully clambered through the gap; the thought of what lay behind them giving each courage to continue. They sat, one behind the other, and the scariest ride either had ever experienced began! Faster and faster, they hurtled down the side of the tower, each leaning in towards the wall for all they were worth. Faster and faster, with Zig holding on tight to Zeeglit's fur and feeling the exhilarating rush of wind on their faces.

In a very short time, they found themselves in a tumbled heap at the foot of the tower – a short distance horizontally, from where they had stood at the arched entrance earlier, but each feeling much older and wiser from their experience. Zeeglit thought of their alternative route and shuddered then, consulting his dimometer, led the way to pick up the thordite track.

Sure enough, they soon found the wide, trodden path and walked for quite some time before sitting down for a rest and a snack by a mound of particularly succulent tuft. As they munched, they recounted their earlier experience but neither was able to shed any light on what the creatures might have been. The bite on Zeeglit's face had left a large red blister which was sore but manageable. They decided to lie down for a short sleep as they were both exhausted from their eventful morning and unsure of what still lay in front of them.

Coming round slowly, Zeeglit became aware of the chill of a fresh breeze and sat up to wake himself fully. Drowsy from sleep, the younger Moogle gazed around. Far in all directions, he could see endless waves of floss, lighter to the west as the sun made its way across the sky, slate-grey in the east with a tell-tale gleam of ice-white still visible in the distance.

With an involuntary shudder, he turned his attention towards the direction the thordite path led. Sitting quietly for a few moments, thinking about what lay ahead of them, Zeeglit slowly became aware of a strange formation drifting towards them.

'Zig. Zig, wake up. Look over there.'

His friend sat up, rubbing his eyes, and tried to focus where Zeeglit pointed. A large, grey shape was drifting towards them just above head height which was very unusual as stray wisps of floss usually travelled at roughly the same level.

As they watched, faint sounds disturbed the airwaves and the pair were intrigued. You might think, mindful of their earlier experience, they would be concerned but moogles have an innocent, compassionate nature, giving them no reason to doubt strangers they may meet.

'Any idea what it is?' enquired Zeeglit.

'Well, I think … Yes, I think it may be a Fog of Whisps. Do you know what they are?'

'I think so. My father told of them once. Aren't they spirits that drift around echoing the last sound they heard?'

'That's right,' replied Zig. 'I have also heard of them but never before seen them as they are only rarely seen on the Altostratus. If we listen carefully, they may help us in our search.'

So they stood and waited for the Fog to drift across. As it drew nearer, they began to see indistinct shapes within the mass: eye sockets with no sight; whispering mouths creating a composition of sounds – high, low, deep, musical and undeniably intriguing.

'Listen,' Zig gasped, suddenly. 'It's Bim!' And Zeeglit could just make out the familiar voice:

'Keep up. Keep up. Keep up …'

As they tuned into the individual whisps, Zeeglit was sure he could pick up the nasal tones he recognised as belonging to thordites and they were convinced they couldn't be too far behind the warrior group as whisps only repeat the last sounds they have heard.

Waiting only until the Fog passed by, the Moogles set off along their path once more, Zig greatly uplifted to hear Bim and spurred on by thoughts that his brother may not be far off; Zeeglit, more worried about what they might soon encounter – preventing Zig from acting rashly and putting himself in danger was going to be a priority as he could never return to

Raylee and Pagloo with news that their third youngster had also been taken and he had promised Ressa not to do anything silly.

Chapter 8
Prisoners at Work

'Get down!' hissed Zig suddenly, dragging Zeeglit behind a raised clump of floss. 'We're not alone!'

Peeping over the top, Zeeglit was grateful that the fur of a moogle offers superb camouflage with their landscape. As you might expect from the high altitude and chilly temperatures, moogles are covered in long shaggy grey and white fur, enabling them to blend in with their background, though some strands of hair sparkle in the sunlight, causing the glistening flickers of light which can be seen through the windows of a whizz-pod.

Some distance in front of them, a thordite camp had been set up and a handful of warriors were lolling around at ease. However, there was no sign of the captive moogles and not enough thordites to be responsible for the wide, well-trodden tracks they had been following.

At first they thought it must be a splinter group that had become separated from the rest but then they saw the group turn to greet another warrior who emerged from a small doorway in an unassuming clump of floss just behind the campsite.

'Let's go!' whispered Zig, enthusiastically, but Zeeglit was rather more cautious.

'No, it's late in the day now and we are tired. If we wait a few hours until night falls, we will find it easier to make our way without being seen. They will not be expecting to be followed and we should be able to get nearer to the entrance and wait for a chance to enter unnoticed,' said Zeeglit, with confidence he was far from feeling.

It wasn't easy to convince Zig that this was the best plan as he was very keen to find his brothers but, reluctantly, had to agree that it made sense. As they waited for the sun to dip over the horizon, they looked carefully for anything that might make their approach easier and decided that they would follow a slight gully that led around to the left of their current position as this might give them a bit of protection.

Several times, Zig suggested they should go but Zeeglit held back until, finally, darkness had fallen and the warriors resting outside the entrance seemed to have fallen asleep, apart from one who was on sentry duty; patrolling around the campsite.

Waiting until the guard had passed their side of the clearing, the two moogles crept cautiously from behind the shrubs and into the gully, where they dropped to their knees and crawled slowly along towards the entrance.

When they were within a few feet of the target, they stopped to look carefully around. They could see the entrance clearly now and it appeared to be a fairly narrow tunnel that twisted to the right just after the entrance. It was impossible to know if there might be any more guards around the bend but there was no sound from within.

Looking back at the thordite patrolling the campsite, they realised he was approaching their position and flattened themselves on the floor of the gully to wait for him to pass by. Once gone, they quietly made a dash for the entrance and moved inside where they were quickly hidden from view.

Communicating only by gestures, they crept alongside the wall towards the bend and cautiously peeped round. However, there appeared to be nothing there other than darkness and they moved on. Moogles have a limited range of visibility in the dark and the two could make out the far side of the tunnel and a few feet ahead of them. However, Zeeglit didn't want to turn on his lamp in case its light could be seen, so they proceeded slowly along the tunnel: Zig leading the way and Zeeglit close behind.

After several metres, the tunnel began to slope downwards. Visibility was slowing them down and as there was no sound of anyone following them, Zeeglit decided to turn on his gantate. Removing the thin, clear crystal tube from his waistcoat pocket, he twisted the base sharply to the left, creating the spark necessary to ignite the hydrogen gas within. Lifting it high, they were able to continue at a much faster pace. The tunnel continued, quite steeply in places and twisted left and right before levelling out and reaching a T-junction. Listening carefully, Zig thought he could hear some faint sounds coming from the right-hand spur so Zeeglit marked their location on his dimometer and they headed along that corridor.

At the end of another hundred metres, they came to another T-junction and again based their route on the faint sounds they could hear. The terrain had changed somewhat from the dry, gritty surface at the entrance and the temperature had dropped by several degrees. Here, the floor underfoot was damp and quite smooth and the walls glistened in the gloom as beads of moisture made their way slowly downward.

Several more corridors followed a similar pattern, two ending in dead ends and the noises they could hear never seemed to get any louder or sound further away. They were beginning to wonder where they were when they became aware of a different sound quite close at hand. Sounding like tiny scurrying feet moving all around them, the two moogles stood together peering into the gloom to see what had come to join them: particularly wary after their earlier encounter in the white tower.

As they stood still and their eyes became more accustomed to their surroundings, they began to catch glimpses of small, spherical creatures; the like of which Zig had never seen before.

'I know what these are,' exclaimed Zeeglit. 'They are Joogs. I saw one once that had fallen from the Altostratus near my home. They burrow through the cloud layers and are thought to protect some great treasure.'

Turning his lamp onto one of the little creatures, they watched in fascination. The small, round body was a mottled blue and silver and glistened with moisture. From underneath, came four feet which swivelled quickly on a central pivot and the little creature, about the size of a tennis ball, scuttled quickly in one direction then the other, disorientated by the bright light. It appeared to have several, individually placed, small eyes on different sides of the sphere and was obviously one of many if the number of feet they could hear was anything to go on. It was also quite apparent that it had no interest in the moogles.

'I wonder what treasure this little fellow knows about?' said Zeeglit. 'It's certainly well-hidden if there's anything down here. Where do you think we are?'

'I don't know,' replied Zig. 'But someone has obviously gone to a lot of trouble to hide something. You wouldn't build a labyrinth like this for no reason. Come on. We need to keep moving; it's cold down here.'

Several tunnels and junctions later they began to notice a blue glow and once more, a definite drop in the temperature. The next T-junction caused them to feel they were on the verge of a discovery: the tunnel to the left looked the same as many they had walked but the one to the right glowed with a beautiful shade of blue; brighter than the sky on a midsummer day.

'This way,' insisted Zig and Zeeglit needed no persuading. Fascinated to see what lay ahead, they hurried towards the ever-brighter glow and, as they rounded a bend, what a sight met their eyes!

Opening out before them was a magnificent cavern. Enormous in size, sunlight bounced off walls of brilliant blue sapphires as it shone in through a large hole in the roof many hundreds of metres above. A few feet ahead of them, a lake of crystal-clear water spread out and, peering down into its depths, they could see it was many metres deep and also lined with the same brilliant sapphires, giving it a truly magical quality. In the depths of the crystal-clear water, a myriad of small creatures darted about and joogs could be seen scurrying about the walls of the cavern.

'Oh wow!' whistled Zig. 'Now I know what the treasure is. But where do we go from here and where is everyone?'

Zeeglit had been studying the cavern carefully and he pointed out a number of entrances to tunnels at varying points high up the walls at the opposite side of the lake.

'I think that is your answer,' he said. 'But I have no idea how we are to get there.' And he sank down on a smooth ledge, set back from the edge of the lake, to take a rest and think what to do next. The thought of retracing their steps and trying some of the many other passages seemed soul-destroying and he felt that they were on the right track yet, at the same time, they seemed to have reached a dead end.

'Can you see any stairs or doorways on this level?' he asked Zig, who was wandering around peering into the distance and looking very frustrated.

'No. Nothing! It's not as if we can jump that high, is it?' he said, frustrated, giving a small leap as if to underline his statement. 'Oh wow! Zeeglit, that's it!'

Standing up, Zeeglit watched in astonishment as his friend jumped higher and higher, lifted by some magical force. Wanting to see for himself, Zeeglit bent his knees and pushed off from the solid blue rock, giving a jump an athlete would have been proud of.

'I don't understand! How can we jump so high?' wondered Zig.

'There must be something in this cavern that makes the difference. I don't understand it but it feels great. Look at me!' replied Zeeglit and gave a jump that would have seemed impossible an hour before.

Side by side on the edge of the underground lake, the pair spent a few moments enjoying their unexpected power before studied the openings in the opposite wall with a newly-found enthusiasm.

'Which one then?' asked Zeeglit.

'I don't know. What if I try and jump near each and see if I can hear or see anything?'

Zeeglit nodded and Zig began to jump. Taking great care to jump straight up so as not to land in the water, Zig jumped higher and higher until he was able to gauge the height and focus on one entrance at a time. After each had been investigated, he returned to Zeeglit and said,

'I think I can hear the sound of voices from the tunnel second from the far end. Do you want to wait here and I will go and investigate?'

'No,' replied Zeeglit, promptly 'We should stick together; there are so many changes of direction. I will have a few practice jumps, then we'll go for it.'

Aiming for targets increasingly higher on the wall behind them, both moogles practiced until they felt confident they could gauge the height of their jump.

'Okay. You go first. But make sure you hang on when you reach the other side,' instructed Zeeglit.

'What if we fall in the water?' queried Zig.

With an involuntary shudder, Zeeglit answered, 'That cannot happen!' A body of water like that which stretched before them was something outside the experience of moogles and swimming was not something they had chance to learn. The thought of being submerged filled him with horror and his chest felt tight with fear as Zig braced himself to jump for the identified ledge.

Giving a magnificent jump that his parents would have been amazed by, Zig landed squarely in the entrance of the tunnel, quickly regaining his balance and turning to wait for Zeeglit.

However, the younger moogle was having serious misgivings. His fear of water was making him feel quite sick and standing so close to such a large lake and knowing that if he didn't jump far enough, he would end up falling into the deep, clear liquid, was nearly enough to make him turn and run. However, knowing he would never be able to live with himself if he let his friends down, he made a supreme effort to pull himself together and prepared to make the jump.

'Come on,' urged Zig, from his lofty position in the tunnel entrance, totally unaware of the pressure Zeeglit was under. 'You can do it. Just jump!'

After a good few minutes talking himself into it, Zeeglit bent his knees and, using his arms for extra momentum, he jumped. He didn't quite make it but managed to grab onto a protruding sapphire just below the ledge on which Zig was standing. Trying not to panic and remembering not to look down, he reached for the paw that was offered from above and felt himself being hauled up to safety.

Lying in an undignified lump at the entrance to the tunnel, Zeeglit felt that he had just aged ten years and had never felt so relieved to feel the firm ground under him.

'That was a close one!' commented Zig, not fully understanding the terror the other moogle had just gone through. 'Are you ready? Let's get going.' And he set off down the tunnel.

Pulling himself to his feet, Zeeglit followed, noting as he went that the walls of this tunnel were quite different from those they had walked through previously. Here, they were studded with sapphires and crystal light bounced ahead of them as it reflected from the gems.

The sounds they had been following were becoming clearer now and they could make out voices, seemingly shouting commands, and the sounds of industry. Realising there may be danger close by, slowly, cautiously, they crept forward, keeping close to the walls on either side.

Rounding a final curve, a much more active sight met their eyes and they could see why the young, strong moogles had been kidnapped.

Laid out below them was a huge cavern, similar to the last, but with one great difference: this one was full of moogles hacking the sapphires from the walls and loading them onto carts. Other moogles were harnessed onto each cart and were pulling these along a track on the far bank towards a tunnel that led off from the opposite corner. There must have been several hundred workers, each dirty and despondent, being kept on task by fifty or so thordites armed with graplars and shouting at their captives.

Sinking down onto their bellies, the moogles peered over their ledge.

'Can you see them?' hissed Zeeglit, straining his eyes to study the sorry individuals before him.

'No, not yet,' came the reply and, for a while, the two lay in silence, each searching for a familiar face.

'I don't think they're here,' said Zig, sadly.

'Let's give it a little longer. There's a lot to take in,' replied Zeeglit, still looking carefully before him.

Suddenly, from an entrance somewhere below where they were perched, a new working party of about twenty entered the cavern, urged on by a handful of thordites. These moogles were clean and immediately the two watchers became more hopeful. Although only the backs of the captives were visible, Zig suddenly grabbed Zeeglit's arm.

'There!' he hissed, pointing to a moogle towards the front of the group. 'That's Bim.'

Although he didn't know him well and was quite some distance above the group, Zeeglit could see at once that this was the case. Bim was fairly tall for a moogle and the fur on the top of his head fell into a natural parting and this was clearly visible now.

'What about Doon?' he asked.

'Not yet, though there are several others from our cluster here.' Despite waiting a while longer, there was no sign of the third brother and they continued to watch as the new group were approached by what appeared to be a senior thordite. He was wearing a dark sash across his body, from which hung a graplar, a lash and another strange, twisted implement that Zeeglit didn't recognise.

Too high to hear what was actually said, it was clear that the group were being given instructions on what was expected. They were then taken to a quiet area of the cavern and some of them began to scrape half-heartedly at the gems in the wall. The thordite task masters shouted at those who were hanging back (a group that included Bim) and pushed them towards the wall. One persistent individual turned and said something to his captor who raised his graplar with intent.

Turning to the wall, the remaining captives began to dig. It wasn't long before it became obvious their paws were hurting and, Zeeglit suspected, bleeding, as they pulled and scraped at the sharp rocks. Too tormenting to watch, they drew back into their tunnel to consider what to do next.

Chapter 9
Zig to the Rescue

'I'm going down there,' said Zig, as soon as they were around the bend.

'No. We need to think this through: if they take you as well, we won't be helping anyone. We need to be careful not to alert the thordites to our presence before we find Doon. And then we have to be able to get out of this labyrinth.'

'I can't just stand by whilst my brothers suffer.'

'I know. But a short while longer won't make much difference,' argued Zeeglit. 'We need to think of a plan before we do anything. Do we just try and free Bim and Doon or do we take all your neighbours or do we try and free everyone?'

'Bim and Doon, obviously. If we free any more, we stand more chance of being noticed. Mind you, there are many more moogles here than thordites – it makes you think they could overthrow their captors if they worked together.'

'It's true,' nodded Zeeglit. 'I hate the thought of leaving so many moogles to suffer but I feel that our first step has to be to save your brothers.'

The debate continued as they talked through different ways to help all the prisoners but they finally decided that they would try and free the brothers and then consider what to do about all the others. Whilst Zeeglit didn't like it, it seemed to make sense for Zig to try and blend in with the working party and get close to Bim as he was of a similar age and his neighbours would recognise him.

One problem was how Zig was to get down the side of the cavern without being seen as he would obviously be spotted if he jumped down from on high. They sat in silence to think about this seemingly impossible problem until Zeeglit came up with an idea:

'What if I create a distraction? If I edge along the ledge away from the tunnel entrance and throw a rock into the far end of the lake, it would give you a few seconds to get to the lower level. I can tuck myself down into the rocks so I can't be seen and you could drop down onto the cavern floor. You would then have to hide until the thordites were looking somewhere else and then creep into the group.'

'I can do that but what do we do then?'

'I think it will be up to you to find out where Doon is and decide if you can get to him or not. If Bim doesn't know where he is, you will just have to jump up here and we'll have to make a run for it then come back for him later.'

Whilst being full of hazards, this was the best plan they could come up with and so the two edged their way back along the corridor. Once back at the entrance, Zeeglit wriggled his way carefully along the narrow ledge that led away from the tunnel. After several painful metres of slithering along the rough shelf, he found a section that was slightly wider and that dipped away from the body of the cavern.

Once safely there, he searched around for a loose gem that he would be able to throw into the lake and then looked back to let Zig know he was ready. Things below seemed to be continuing smoothly so, on an agreed signal – Zig gave a clear nod of his head – Zeeglit raised the rock and let it fly as hard as he could, towards the far end of the lake.

The loud splash was unexpected and created the hoped-for chaos down below. Thordites, unsure of what was happening, shouted louder at their captives as if they were somehow responsible and there was a buzz of excitement amongst the workers as they too wondered what was happening.

Taking advantage of the distraction, Zig slipped quietly over the edge and let himself drop onto the floor several metres below before quickly scuttling to hide in a convenient crevice in the cavern wall. Hoping he had not been noticed, he fought to control his erratic breathing and waited for the excitement to die down.

The leader of the thordites gave a command for silence and, after a short while, when nothing moved and silence filled the air, he seemed to decide that there was nothing to worry about and announced that a stray rock must have fallen from the roof of the cavern so work was resumed.

Waiting on the ledge above until normal work started again, Zeeglit then edged his way slowly back to the tunnel and peered carefully over. After a short while, he gasped quietly then held his breath as he saw his companion slowly making his way around the cavern wall towards his brother.

Twice he had to duck back into the shadows as thordites walked in his direction but luck was on his side and, on his third attempt, he managed to reach the group and blend in. Zeeglit could see the startled recognition of some of the group as they realised who he was but they quickly turned back to their task to cover his tracks. Pretending to work like the rest,

Zig dug sapphires from the wall and placed them in a waiting truck; each time making his way closer to his brother as he returned to the rock face.

After a dozen or so stones, he at last came within reach of Bim.

'Don't look round!' he whispered.

Close beside him, he felt Bim stiffen.

'You! How? Did they get you as well?'

'No,' replied Zig. 'We've come to get you. Where's Doon?'

'Quiet over there!' came the nasal tones of one of the thordite over-seers. 'Get on with it or there will be no rest for you tonight.'

In silent agreement, the brothers worked side-by-side for a while before Bim took the chance to whisper, 'Look at the cart.'

Turning to look at the track behind them, Zig finally saw Doon. Harnessed to the front of the next cart in line was the third brother.

'We have to go now,' Zig spoke with a quiet insistence and he took a large gemstone towards the waiting cart. Dropping his heavy blue rock into the back, Zig was relieved to see Bim following with another and he edged his way around towards the harness.

He had just managed to unhook the first rope from the truck when he was spotted; both by the closest thordite, several feet away, and Doon.

'Hey, you! Get back!' demanded the snarling face of the over-seer as he started towards the brothers.

'Quick, Bim. Help me get this off,' shouted Zig and they pulled at the harness as fast as they could.

However, it was not easy and their enemy was approaching fast.

'Hurry,' said Doon, unable to help and keeping a close eye on what was happening.

Zeeglit also watched helplessly from above as more thordites, alerted by the sound of shouting, came running to see what was happening. Knowing he could do nothing but watch, Zeeglit felt sure there was no chance when another movement caught his eye: the crowd of workers nearby had decided to help and, at the last moment, they rushed at the thordite closest to the brothers and over-powered him.

At the same moment, the ropes slid from Doon's shoulders and he stood up. Zeeglit stood up too.

'Trust me and jump!' shouted Zig, and hoping they would follow his lead, he jumped for the tunnel where Zeeglit waited, now poised to run.

Not understanding what was happening, Bim and Doon followed their brother's lead and jumped for the ledge, leaving a fight raging below as the thordites struggled to regain control of their prisoners. Landing unsteadily, they were grabbed by the waiting moogles and the four began to run down the corridor. It was difficult at first, until their eyes became accustomed to the darkness but they kept close together and Zeeglit led the way with his dimometer in his paw, the small amount of light from his gantate illuminating a few metres in front of them.

At each turn in the corridor, he read the dial and made a swift decision: a left turn then a right, another to the right and still the four ran on. Feeling sure they must be being followed, they wasted no time to look behind and no breath to speak. Fear helped to push them forward and they rushed on in the gloom, bumping shoulders on jagged rocks and stumbling over the uneven surface.

However, as one tunnel followed another, Zeeglit became even more worried: the ground was definitely sloping downward and that just wasn't right. Zig was apparently also thinking the same thing because he caught Zeeglit by the arm and, just for a moment, they stopped.

Breathing heavily and studying the dimometer with care, Zeeglit had to admit he must have made a mistake.

'I'm sorry. I don't know where, but I have made a wrong turn. We have headed too far east and this doesn't feel right at all.'

'It's not your fault,' said Bim, generously. 'It's dark and you've had to make split second decisions. I'm sure I would have made errors too. Can you tell where we have to go now?'

'I feel there is no alternative at the moment. The thordites must be somewhere behind us. I suggest we keep going until we come to a junction then assess the route from there.'

They all agreed with Zeeglit's plan and set off again at a jog, but a little slower this time as there were no sounds of anyone in close pursuit. The nature of their surroundings was now changing quite considerably. Going deeper into the cloud, the walls that had been damp were now dripping and the air smelt dank and musty.

On they went, each becoming increasingly concerned and increasingly wet as the water dripped heavily until it was like running through a heavy shower and their wet fur clinging to their faces made it even harder to see where they were going. The tunnel was also becoming narrower and Zeeglit had a very bad feeling about their situation, never mind the amount of water he was now running through!

Then, suddenly, their race was over: stretched across the width of the tunnel in front of them was a mesh gate. Turning quickly round, they were just in time to see a similar gate slide down from the roof behind them and they realised why there had been no sounds of anyone following them. There had been no need. They had run straight into a trap.

'Thought you would get away, did you? Well, there's no way out of here!' A heavily set thordite warrior approached the other side of the mesh. 'Make yourselves comfortable for the night,' he sneered. 'We'll be back for you in the morning.' And, with that, he turned around and disappeared back from where he had come.

'Well, that's that then!' said Doon, despondently.

'We will find a way, brother,' Bim tried to reassure him but looked to Zeeglit for support. 'Any ideas?'

But Zeeglit was looking rather sorry for himself as he thought about staying for even a few more minutes in this very watery place and could offer him no hope.

Turning back to Zig he said, 'Well, it was certainly a surprise to see you. How is father?'

Zig explained about the beating their father had taken at the hands of the warriors and both Bim and Doon were angry and very worried. Going on to explain about the help given to him and their neighbours by Ressa's healing powers did give them some comfort and they thanked Zeeglit for trying to come to their rescue without his father.

Their next action was to examine the mesh gates at either end of their prison. Made of an unknown thread wound through strong metal bars, there was no way to break through them and they fitted tightly against the tunnel walls, making it impossible to squeeze past.

Deciding they really were trapped and they needed to try and get some sleep, they explored their narrow cell and found that most of the water was dripping from the top of the tunnel and running down the middle so, if they sat alongside one of the walls, they could keep most of their body dry. Still feeling very sorry for himself, and also very angry at his own mistakes, Zeeglit sat at the end of the small group and sulked whilst Zig told the tale of all that they had seen since they had left Raylee and Pagloo in the family burrow.

Shocked and amazed, Bim and Doon listened as Zig told his fascinating tale of the glums, the fallen star and the beautiful tower with its deadly secret and the journey to the sapphire caverns. They also discussed the amazing sapphire caverns and tried to guess, unsuccessfully, what the thordites might want the gems for. Then, knowing there was no way they could make a plan for the morning and realising how tired they actually were, they made themselves as comfortable as possible (which was not very comfortable at all) and tried to rest. Zeeglit's last thoughts before he dropped off were of his family and, for the first time, he wondered if he would ever see them again.

Despite their dreadful surroundings, they must have had some sleep as sounds from along the tunnel woke them rudely in the morning. Heavy footsteps of approaching thordite warriors had them scrambling to their feet. Bim moved in front to protect his brothers and Zeeglit, never one to be in a bad mood for long, moved alongside him.

'A good night's sleep?' the thick set individual from the night before laughed. Then, turning to the thordite on his right, he instructed, 'Open the gate – let's have them out of here.'

'Where are you taking us?' asked Zig, making an effort to sound a lot more confident than he actually felt.

'You'll find out soon enough,' was the only reply he got before the mesh was raised and warriors moved forward to grab the four moogles roughly and march them along the tunnel.

Short legs hurrying to keep up with the longer ones of their captors, the moogles were part marched, part dragged along too many tunnels to remember. They had travelled upwards at the start and Zeeglit was heartily relieved that they were back in a much drier area although that was really little comfort.

Aware that it was getting lighter and that there were sounds of voices from up ahead, Zeeglit began to pay more attention. A few more twists and turns and the group entered a completely different area. A much wider corridor ran straight towards an imposing entrance about ten metres away and it was towards this archway that they were now led.

Along the edge of this area there were small circular pods where groups of thordites stopped what they were doing to watch the little band walk past. They seemed to be relaxing as they were lounging around on comfortable cushions and seemed happy and at ease.

The roof was punctuated by a series of holes allowing natural light to enter and the air was fresh and very welcome. The entrance before them was quite splendid yet seemed unnecessarily tall. There were two smooth columns of crystal at each side and across the top was an arch of the same material, carved with scenes of thordite activity.

As they approached this magnificent portal, the guards stopped to exchange words with sentries posted in front of a crystal pillar, giving time for the moogles to get their breath back and take in their surroundings.

Trying to make out what was depicted above the arch, Zeeglit slowly began to realise the purpose behind the sapphire mining. Well aware that the gems created some sort of magical atmosphere enabling the moogles to jump to extraordinary heights, he realised he was looking at images showing this power put to use.

The first pictures seemed to show gems being fed into a huge machine. These were followed by others showing what looked to be a gas coming from the other end and being syphoned into special canisters. Thordites, with these special packs strapped to their backs were then shown flying above the cloud surface and some appeared to be moving towards the Cirrostratus and the planets beyond.

Looking behind, he could see the others also taking in this information and he wondered what they would find through the doorway. Walking underneath, they entered a large chamber with many groups of thordites standing around talking and, on a raised platform at the far end, a group sat around in deep conversation. Eyes focussed on this group, the moogles realised this was where they were heading.

At the head of the group was a very imposing figure indeed. This thordite was dressed in long blue robes and was very definitely female – the first they had seen in the caverns. She was also, very obviously, the most important thordite in the room. As they drew close, she stopped her conversation and turned ice-white eyes upon the captives.

'Moogles!' she hissed, this one word being enough to show her dislike of the species. 'Why are they here?' she asked the leader of their guards.

'Begging your pardon, Isilit, this is the group who tried to escape from the mine last night. We trapped them in the lower levels.'

'Why have you brought them to me? Just put them back to work.'

'I would normally but two of them were not our captives. They haven't had their fur clipped. This means they have entered the caverns by themselves and there may be more.'

Zeeglit and Zig were pushed forward and they were turned to reveal the long hair on the back of their necks which they hadn't noticed had been cut on the others. As the eyes of all on the platform focussed on them, they felt waves of hatred coming towards them. This was sinister. This was threatening. And Zeeglit felt very afraid.

'What are you doing here? Where did you come from?' asked Isilit.

His voice little more than a whisper, Zeeglit tried to explain himself. 'Well, we came to …'

'Speak up!' demanded Isilit.

With a sudden rush of anger, Zeeglit cleared his throat and tried again. 'I came to get my friends back. You have no right to take them!'

'No right! You dare to tell me I have no right! I have no care for your rights, little creature!' Then, turning to the guard, she continued, 'Put them back to work.' And with that she turned back to her companions and the moogles had been dismissed.

'You can't do that!' shouted Zeeglit.

But it was no good. She did not turn back and the guards began to drag the four back out of the chamber.

Looking wildly around him, Zeeglit suddenly focussed on a familiar face. At the side of the huge chamber, sat a small group of eight or so thordites, deep in conversation and dressed in fine tunics indicating their high rank. At the side of the group now facing him, was Blauron.

Sure, it was the same leader who had spoken to his father recently, Zeeglit called out, 'Blauron! Over here!'

Zeeglit wasn't sure who was the most surprised: his fellow moogles or the guards; all of whom wondered how he came to call a senior thordite by name.

Surprised by the shout, the thordite leader looked up. The guards stopped for a second, unsure what to do and Blauron beckoned the group to come over. Standing before this group was almost as terrifying as the other but Zeeglit knew this was his only chance to speak out.

'Please. Can you help us like my father helped you?' he asked clearly but simply.

'What is happening here?' Blauron asked the guards and he was given a quick recount of the tale. When the guard had finished speaking, Blauron stood up.

'Well, little moogle, it seems you have got yourself into a lot of trouble. What do you have to say for yourself?'

'I am only trying to save my friends and take them back to their parents who are very worried about their situation.' Knowing that Blauron had shown great concern and tenderness for his own daughter, Zeeglit pursued his point. 'Their father has taken a severe beating and they are needed back at home to care for the family. You have many other workers here: two would not be missed.'

'Every worker is valuable to our cause,' stated Blauron. 'However, I am aware that I am in your father's debt and I do not like that. Stay here for a moment and I will see what can be done.'

So saying, he moved towards the far end of the room and was soon deep in conversation with Isilit. Even from where they were standing, several metres away, they could tell there was a big argument going on. The guards surrounding the moogles, whispered together and Bim, who was standing closest to Zeeglit, sidled over.

'What's going on? How do you know that creature?'

'We met a short while ago. Ressa saved his daughter.'

'He owes you?'

'I hope so.'

Seeing Blauron coming back down the hall, the guards quickly jerked the two moogles apart and stood to attention. Reaching their side, Blauron spoke to the guards.

'You are ordered to release these four into my custody. Isilit has authorised it.'

Confused, and wary of making the wrong move, the guards looked from one to another and back along the room to where their magnificent ruler stood glowering down the hall. A small nod in their direction convinced them that she had, indeed, given permission.

As the guards stood back, Blauron turned to Zeeglit. 'Quick. Follow me before she changes her mind,' and he turned and walked towards the entrance to the chamber.

Needing no encouragement, the moogles scurried to keep up with the long legs striding rapidly ahead of them.

'Can we trust him?' asked Doon, as quietly as he could.

'Do you have a choice?' came the throaty reply from Blauron.

Head held high, eyes facing forward, Blauron led the group back through the wide corridor with off-duty over-seers watching their progress. As they passed back under the great arch, he turned right, then shortly right again, before reaching a straight corridor, leading into the distance. Turning back to face the group, he spoke to the three brothers.

'You are very lucky to have such a friend. If it was not for this moogle's father, I would no longer have a daughter. His bravery and compassion have secured your release. However, if you are ever caught again, you will not be so lucky. No captives have ever before been released or escaped.'

Then, turning to Zeeglit, he added, 'Your father and I are now even. Do not be fooled: I am not your friend but I did owe him and I always pay my debts. Today you have made a very powerful enemy – Isilit is our high chieftain and has a strong dislike of all moogles but she will not forget you. Make sure she never has cause to see you again! At the end of this corridor, you will find a concealed exit. Do not look back!' And with that, he turned and was gone.

Not waiting to be told twice, the four moogles followed Zeeglit until they felt the fresh air of the outdoors on their faces and they found themselves outside the labyrinth with no thordite warriors in sight.

'Which way now?' asked Doon.

Consulting his dimometer, Zeeglit only took a few seconds to decide: 'If we head east for a while, we should reach that ridge over there then we can stop for a rest.' They did this in silence; each full of their own thoughts and hardly daring to believe they were going to make their escape without being followed.

However, they reached the ridge with no signs of pursuit and, once over the top, they flopped onto the floor and began to believe they might actually be free. Rolling over onto his belly, Zig said what all the brothers were thinking:

'Well, Zeeglit, tell us the story.'

So Zeeglit told the brothers what he and Ressa had been returning to their home to tell them three long days before. Listening in silence until he had finished his tale, the young moogles realised how lucky they had indeed been: to have seen Blauron on their way out of the grand hall was some sort of miracle and that he was an honourable thordite was very welcome surprise.

Chapter 10
An Alien Invader

Realising that it was now late morning and they were still relatively close to the thordite mines, they decided that they needed to make a plan and move on. It was clear that they could do nothing to help the other moogle captives at this time, so Zeeglit marked their position on his dimometer for the future. He then explained an idea that had been growing in his mind since he had first seen the glums: he knew that he had to try to do something about the fallen star for the sake of the floss harvest in his home neighbourhood.

It didn't take long for the brothers to think about this and agree that they would help in any way they could although they couldn't imagine what they would be able to do. Having agreed, they stood up again and, following directions from Zeeglit's dimometer, they set off at a steady pace; glad to be putting distance between themselves and their terrible ordeal.

There was no sign of the white tower as they made their way towards the position of the fallen star and it was late in the day that they began to hear the distant moans of the glums. However, another strange sound also reached their ears. A high-pitched muttering could clearly be heard coming from somewhere to the left of the track and, filled with curiosity, the group decided a short detour was worth it. Moving slowly and carefully, they headed towards the origin of the sound.

'Stop!' shouted Zeeglit. 'Look!'

A short distance in front of them, the surface began to slope quite steeply and they realised they were at the rim of a sink-hole. This formation occurs when a twisting wind whips the vapour within the cloud into an icy spiral that tapers down to a low point; too slippery to climb out from. Peering carefully down into the hole, the moogles could just make out the source of the muttering.

'What's that?' asked Doon, intrigued by the small, dark creature trying unsuccessfully to scale the smooth icy sides of its prison.

'I have no idea,' said Zeeglit, but it seems to need our help. 'Hey, you. Up here.'

The movement below stopped and the strangest little face was turned towards them. Two beady black eyes, fixed close together in a small, wrinkled face regarded Zeeglit intently. Long, thin arms extended from the side of its squat little body and its hands rested on the floor alongside two paws, very different in nature from a moogle's, having two clear toes on each,

With its head on one side, the creature began to speak very quickly in a high, squeaky voice,

'Oh, lucky, lucky me. You have been destined to find me. Thank you, thank you, thank you. How will you get me out?'

'We'll have to have a minute to think about it,' answered Zeeglit and the moogles sat down to think.

'The main thing has to be that we don't end up joining this strange fellow at the bottom of the sink hole,' said Bim.

'I agree,' said Zeeglit. 'We need something we can offer down for it to grab. Any ideas?'

'What if we use your waistcoat?' suggested Zig. 'I'm sure the creature can't be very heavy.'

'Great idea: let's give it a go,' agreed Bim, and Zeeglit slipped out of his clothing and handed it to Bim.

Lying down at the edge of the hole, Bim peered over. 'Right: I need you to catch on to this and I'll pull you up,' he shouted.

Lowering the waistcoat into the hole, Bim watched as the strange creature tried to reach up for the cloth. However, it was unable to stretch far enough and after a short time he realised it wasn't going to work so, shouting down that he would be back in a moment, he pulled the material up and turned back to the others.

'It's close but not close enough. We'll have to think again.'

'You could hold onto my feet and lower me down the side to grab it,' suggested Zig.

'I don't like it,' said Doon.

'Neither do I,' agreed Bim, but had to admit he couldn't think of anything else and couldn't imagine walking away and leaving the creature at the bottom of the sink-hole.

So it was, that Zig, held firmly around his ankles by his oldest brother, edged his way down the side of the slippery ice, holding out the waistcoat towards the waiting creature. In turn, Zeeglit and Doon lay on their fronts and gripped Bim in a similar fashion – it did go through Zeeglit's head that they would look very strange if anyone saw them from above!

Muttering constantly, the little creature below jumped up and down excitedly and tried to grab the extended cloth. As

110

Zig came within reach, he felt a tug on the waistcoat as the creature caught hold and scrabbled over it and tiny fingers formed a vice-like grip around his own. He shouted for Bim to pull them up. This was not difficult to do as the creature weighed very little and before long they were sat at the top of the hole facing each other. Seen close to, the creature was every bit as strange as they had first thought.

'Thank you. Oh, thank you! I thought I was to end my days in that hole.' Looking at Zig with adoration, the stranger continued, 'I am yours. You saved me and now I am yours. Wherever you go, I go. Whatever you need, I will do.'

'There's no need for that,' replied Zig with embarrassment. 'I only did what anyone would do.'

'No. You saved me and our law decrees that I am now indebted to you. I will be forever by your side.'

Realising how awkward his brother was finding this but actually finding it quite amusing, Doon asked the question that was on all their minds: 'What are you? I mean, where do you come from?'

'I am a gibberwit, and you can call me Gib. That is not my name but it is easier to say,' the stranger replied. 'We are a race of intergalactic travellers. I arrived in your homeland a few days ago and after only a few hours, I slipped and found myself trapped as you first saw me.'

'Are you on your own?' asked Zeeglit, fascinated by his first sight of this new species.

'I am. We always travel alone. Our purpose is to find out about the galaxy and report back.'

'But where are you from and how did you get here?' asked Bim.

'My home is many light years from here. I hitched a lift on a passing space shuttle as it left the moon and dropped off here as it went past. It looked like a good place to be.'

'Well, you are welcome to come with us for a while,' offered Bim.

'Oh, I certainly will. Wherever he goes, I will too,' he replied, gesturing to Zig.

'Well, for now,' said Bim awkwardly. 'Anyway, I guess we'd better get back on the route.'

Nodding in agreement, they stood up and began to retrace their steps to the path they had left earlier.

'Well, this is good. I wonder where we are going. What do you think we will see? It is good to have company for a while,' babbled Gib.

'We are going to take a look at something we saw earlier,' Zig answered the question and explained once again about the fallen star and the glums.

'Oh my, oh my. That is indeed a disaster. This is something I would like to see. Which way do we go?'

'Well, we are going the right way now,' answered Zeeglit, slightly confused.

'That is good. Well, what will we see on the way? How long will it take to get there?'

'It won't take too long.'

'Oh, that is good. How long? Which way do we go now? What else will I see?'

Beginning to wish they had left the small gibberwit at the bottom of the sink-hole, Zeeglit ignored this latest series of questions and concentrated on his dimometer.

Scurrying along on its hands and feet, Gib stayed close behind Zig and continued his barrage of questions. Zig answered as best he could for a while but he too began to tire of the constant gibbering and found himself trying to put some space between him and his new shadow. Finding it very amusing, Doon teased his brother quietly but Zig did not see the funny side.

'Stop it,' ordered Bim. 'Just concentrate on where we're going.' And the group continued on their way towards the moaning that was now growing clearer with a constant stream of questions and inane statements from the newcomer.

Despite having been told the story of the fallen star, Bim and Doon were not prepared for the strange site that met their eyes as they came over the ridge and saw the glums sitting around the singed floss and even Gib was quiet for a moment. In the now gathering gloom of the evening, the mournful creatures looked exactly as Zeeglit and Zig had last seen them and Zeeglit doubted they had moved at all.

'Well, well. What have we here?' asked Gib, unnecessarily. 'What can be done? What will I see next?'

Ignoring this, Zig suggested they stop there for the night. 'We can't do anything in the dark and I think this would be an easy place to carve out a shelter.'

The others agreed. No one felt thordites would be a problem with the magnificent figures of the glums so close by and before long they had dug a shallow tunnel and sleeping chamber to shelter from the chill night air. For the first time in a while Zeeglit felt rather hungry but there didn't appear to be any floss nearby so there was nothing to be done.

However, it appeared he wasn't the only one.

'Has anyone got anything to eat?' asked Zig.

'Of course not: you'd know if we had,' answered Doon. 'We're all hungry but there's no food near here.'

Gib, had been sitting as close as he was allowed to Zig but now he jumped up. 'You are hungry, Zig? I will get you food. What do you eat? Where will it be?'

'We eat tuft. Do you know it? It grows on shrubs all over the place, only not here!'

'I do not know it but I am sure I can find some.' And, with that, he disappeared down the tunnel.

'Phew!' whistled Zig, flopping onto his back. 'He's exhausting!'

'He certainly is and he's all yours!' Doon joked.

'Stop it you two. He's very kind to go and get food,' chided Bim. 'Mind you, I don't know how far he'll have to go to find some and I suppose he may not find his way back.'

'Do you think so?' asked Zig hopefully.

Bim just glared at his younger brother and they all lay back to wait. In reality, it wasn't long before they heard a scurrying in the tunnel and Gib reappeared with his tiny arms laden with succulent tuft and the moogles were all very grateful.

'What do you eat, Gib?' asked Zeeglit, curiously.

'As we travel all over the skies and never know what our next meal will be, we have developed the ability to eat just about anything. I tried a bit of your tuft as I was collecting it and it will do just fine,' he replied and they all began to tuck in to the meal he had provided.

As they ate, they talked of their adventures that day and Gib kept up a constant barrage of questions: some of which they answered and some they didn't. Then, as soon as they had finished eating, a strange thing happened: Gib suddenly said, 'I rest now,' and he appeared to shut down. He didn't curl up to sleep, he just dropped his head down onto his chest, closed his eyes and that was that.

'Do you think he's alright?' asked Zig.

'I think it must just be his way,' said Zeeglit. 'He seems very peaceful.'

So the moogles stayed where they were and began to make plans for the next day.

'I think that we will have to go our separate ways,' Zeeglit began. 'I know our parents will need to know we are safe but I have to try to do something about the fallen star. I am sure this is the cause of the problems in my homeland.'

'You're right,' agreed Bim. 'I want to see my father and find out how he is. We also need to let our neighbours know what has happened to their young and try and think of a way to rescue them. However, I don't like to think of you continuing on your own.'

'He won't have to.' Zig joined the discussion to say that he had decided to go with Zeeglit. As long as their parents saw his brothers to reassure themselves that they were ok, he was sure they wouldn't mind if he went with the other moogle to see if he could help and, besides, he was really rather enjoying their adventures. Bim and Doon agreed with this and Zeeglit was very pleased to have the company for a while longer. He had no idea how he was going to tackle his problem but it would be good to have someone to talk it through with and he felt that he and Zig had made a good team since they had set out together two days earlier.

Then there was the question of Gib.

'What are we going to do with it?' asked Zig, pointing to the stationary creature.

'Are you joking?' said Doon. 'It's not our choice – he will just go wherever you go. You heard him.'

'He can't stay with me forever,' said Zig. 'He must go home sometime.'

'I'm sure he will, but for now I think Doon is right: he will go with us,' said Zeeglit. 'Who knows; maybe he'll know what to do.' And on that note, they decided to settle down for the night and think again in the morning when they were fresher.

Chapter 11
A Plan Is Made

Tired out from their adventures of the day, the moogles all slept well and when they woke up it was a lovely bright morning and Gib was sitting in the entrance to the burrow finishing off the last of the tuft. Making their way outside they all enjoyed a roll in the morning dew and a few moments grooming their fur: a regular way for a moogle to begin its day, before they sat once again to talk of their plans and explain to Gib what they had decided.

'I will go wherever you go and do whatever you need me to do,' Gib told Zig. 'Where will we go first? What can I do? What will I see?' and he was off on a stream of never-ending questions.

'Oh no, I don't think I can put up with this all day,' said Zig, beginning to panic.

'You'll get used to it. We'll give it things to do and think about to keep it occupied,' answered Zeeglit. 'Hey Gib: any idea how we can make things right for this star?'

Gib turned and looked thoughtful. 'Hmm, you ask me. I like that. I will think.' And he began to pace backwards and forwards a short way off.

After watching him talking to himself for a few moments, the others looked towards the area where the glums sat mourning their secret. If you didn't know, you would never guess what secret they were hiding, it being so well buried under the scree.

'I think you two should be on your way,' said Zeeglit. 'Your parents will be so relieved to see you.'

'I would like to have been able to tell them what your plans are,' he replied. 'We will wait a short while longer to see if we can come up with …'

'I know! I know! Gib will save the day!' came a sudden, shrill screech. 'We will put it back. We will take it home!'

'Sorry? Who will? How?' asked Zig. 'In case you haven't noticed we can't fly and that thing will be very heavy!'

'No, no, no. I will call for my friends and they will come in their flying machines and put it back.'

Fascinated, and wondering if this really was a possibility, they all crowded around their tiny friend and began to quiz him about his idea:

'How can you contact your friends?'

'Can they really carry a star?'

'How would you know where it goes?'

'How would they carry it?'

'Enough,' he silenced them, putting up a hand. 'I can call for help if ever I need to.'

'Well why didn't you ask them to help you get out of the hole?' asked Doon doubtfully.

'I would have done if it had become desperate but I had not given up hope of getting out of there and we only call for help if it's an emergency. This is. We know the galaxy so well, I am sure we can work out where this star has fallen from. We will just have to work out a way of fastening the star to the spaceships and we will be fine.'

Feeling cheered by the positive way in which Gib spoke, Zeeglit turned to Bim. 'I think it is now time for you to go,' he said again.

'This time I agree with you. Come, Doon.' Then turning to his youngest brother, he warned, 'Don't do anything that is too dangerous. We need you to come home to us.'

'I'll be fine,' he assured him. 'I'll be back before you know it and I can help you rescue the others from the mine. Wait for me.'

Zeeglit and Zig stood to watch the two brothers making their way along the track home whilst Gib jumped up and down, impatient to get on with the task of replacing the star. As they disappeared round the bend, they turned and gave a final wave.

'Right, how will we begin? What shall we do first?'

'I think we need to take another look at the star and think about how it could be lifted, if you really think your friends can help,' Zeeglit replied.

Almost beside itself with excitement, the little gibberwit set off towards the glums with the other two following.

'Do you really think he has a plan?' Zig asked quietly.

'I don't know but I don't have any other ideas at the moment and he sounded very sure. I think we'll just have to go along with him for now and hope he's right. What we need to think about now is how the star can be lifted out of the hole and carried back into the sky if they do come for it.'

Reaching the circle of glums and the area of singed floss, Zeeglit called a greeting to the motionless guardians but they gave no sign of having heard him and continued with their soulful groaning. Gib continued his steady string of questions and statements and followed the moogles to the area where the star was lying.

Gently, once again, Zeeglit began to move the floss aside to look at the dull star beneath and he was worried that the rhythmic vibrations coming from it were weaker than a few days before. Diving into the large hole created by the star's impact, Gib stopped, looked, whistled and then busied around, looking and touching. Zig joined Zeeglit at the edge of the crash site and they lay on the floss to think about what they should do next.

Appearing at their side, however, Gib was the one with the answers: 'First I will call my friends. This is definitely something they need to help with. This is an emergency. Then we will get some rope to make a net for them to lift the star.'

'But where will we get rope?' asked Zig.

'Well, I know where thread is created,' answered Zeeglit. 'My father has told me of the place and we could get some woven into rope but it is a very long way from here.'

'How far?' asked Zig.

'The moon-spiders spin strong, fine thread at the polar regions. There are traders who carry their products from place to place but you never know where they are going to be and they wouldn't have enough for what we need anyway,' Zeeglit replied.

'By the time we got there and back it would be too late anyway,' said Zig.

'I know a way we can travel there – it's very exciting: very fast but it should be safe. Getting back will be more difficult. But we do need a strong net if this star is to be moved.'

'How can we get there?' asked Zig.

'We can travel on the Jet Stream. Its narrow air currents move around the Polar Regions in great loops and I believe one arc passes quite close to this area. We could jump onto a cloud within this jet of air as it passes, then jump off as it nears the North Pole. The only problem is that it travels from west to east so it would be good for getting there but no good for the return journey.'

'Wow! That does sound exciting,' agreed Zig. 'So how do you contact your friends, Gib?'

'I will show you now,' he said. 'But first you must fill your ears with floss.'

Breaking off the softest top layers of the floss within reach, the two moogles did as they were told. Then, motioning for them to stay where they were, Gib moved a few metres away. Standing with his head thrown back and his arms raised to the heavens above, he let out a long, shrill, piercing whistle. Just for a second, the glums stopped their moaning and five pale moon faces turned towards the gibberwit. The first whistle was followed by a series of long and short blasts then silence. The glums resumed their vigil and Gib returned to his friends. Taking the floss from their ears, Zig asked.

'Was that it? What now? When will they come?'

Zeeglit laughed: 'You sound like him with all those questions.'

'It will take a long while – several times the sun will rise and set before they arrive but we have to go now to get the rope so we are back when they get here. Which way do we go?' he asked Zeeglit.

Looking at his dimometer, Zeeglit pointed out the route: a path leading away from the direction of the sapphire caverns, and the little party set off in that direction. Keeping up his now familiar barrage of questions, Gib scurried alongside them, eager to learn about their life on the clouds and they talked of things they could see and things they thought would be of interest to a visitor from another world.

By the time the sun had travelled half way across the sky, they could see a great arch of grey floss in the distance and Zeeglit explained that it marked one of the entrances to the Jet Stream. Looming up above them, it looked very imposing as they approached and they were almost level with its walls before they noticed the individual standing underneath.

'Ah, the guardian of the gate,' said Zeeglit, knowingly. 'Hi-lo. I believe you know my father: Ressa of the Valley of Nimbo. It's been a long time since he was last here but he has told me about you.'

Peering from under a long tangled matt of fur, the sentry studied Zeeglit carefully before breaking out in a wide grin. Zig had just realised that the guardian was female before he was drawn forward to be introduced.

'Zig, Gib, I would like you to meet Magitail. She has been the guardian of the gate for as long as anyone can remember and has helped my father out of a scrape on more than one occasion.' Seeing that Gib was about to ask questions, he hurried on to explain the reason for their journey today and Magitail nodded in agreement when he checked if they would be able to reach the North Pole via this route. Yet when she opened her mouth to speak, Zeeglit was totally and unexpectedly captivated. Her voice was like a series of tinkling bells and made him wonder about her age, though he knew better than to ask.

'You will be able to reach the Pole but need to take a while to adjust to the darkness before you travel. At this time of year, there is no daylight at the Pole and you will be unable to see well enough to make your landing if you have not prepared. Come sit with me and we will share stories as you wait for your eyes to adjust.'

So saying, she led the party to sit within a chamber carved into the great wall of the arch and provided each with a soft black strip of fabric which she fastened carefully around their head to cover their eyes. It was very surreal to sit in darkness in this unusual place with this strange group yet Zig felt completely at ease. He listened as Magitail caught up on stories of Ressa and reminisced about events from the past, giving Zeeglit an insight into his father as a much younger moogle who had obviously enjoyed more than his fair share of adventures.

Gib also listened quietly: whether it was the sense of peace created by Magitail's musical voice, confusion caused by the sudden darkness of the blindfold or sheer interest in the stories, he couldn't tell but they passed a very relaxing hour and Zig was disappointed when the guardian finally announced that they were ready. As the blindfolds were removed, the three were led through to the inside of the arch and the travellers found themselves looking at a very different scene.

They were nearing the edge of a cliff of floss and way, way below he could see a huge area of blue on the Oodle Pool, flecked with white horses. They could feel the wind whipping up as they approached the edge and Zig felt the need to grip Gib's hand as he was worried the little creature may be blown over the edge. They could see small clumps of floss dotted about within the air stream whizzing past very fast (several carrying other moogles) and whilst the ride looked exciting, he had no idea how they were supposed to climb aboard one of these ships as to jump would have been impossible.

Meanwhile, Magitail was explaining to Zeeglit how to manage the ride, where to aim for and what to do when they reached their destination. They watched her take a long pole with a hook on the end from where it lay on the floor and she stood in wait at the edge of the cliff.

'Be ready to jump when I say,' said Magitail and they stood poised for action, Zig and Gib still holding tightly to one another.

'Ready,' warned Magitail as she eyed a potential clump of floss and then, bringing the pole down suddenly and skilfully, she managed to hook it and draw it into the side. Zeeglit could see the Jet Stream tugging at it and when she shouted, 'Jump!' he moved quickly and they were off: three hardy travellers, whisked along at an exhilarating speed to who knows where.

'Wee-hee!' shouted Gib and Zig laughed out loud with excitement as they raced along at high speed. Their boat was only just big enough for three yet they felt to be in no danger of falling off as the floss beneath their feet was deep and spongy, giving them good grip which was a good thing with the speed the wind was whipping past their ears. Cliffs of floss flashed past, as did the landscape way below and it was no time before it became dark and Zig could see why they had to be prepared for this drastic change from day to night.

'We'll be there very soon,' shouted Zeeglit, trying to make himself heard above the wind.

'But how do we get off?' asked Zig, wondering if there would be another guardian with a pole at the end of their journey.

'Wait and see,' replied Zeeglit mysteriously and Zig waited, intrigued as he watched his friend taking off his waistcoat. As the glimmer of ice up ahead indicated they were getting close to a Polar cliff of ice floss (the north being particularly cold) Zeeglit stood tall and, using his body as a mast and his waistcoat as a sail, he steered their craft skilfully alongside the ice. Immediately, the three jumped quickly to safety before the ship of white floss sailed gaily on its way.

'Well done, well done,' said Gib, respectfully. 'I could not have done that better myself,' and both moogles covered a smile for fear of offending him. Turning away from the drop into darkness behind them, the questions began again: 'Now we are here, where do we go next? How will we know where to find these moon-spiders? Will we even be able to see them if they are nearby?'

'Magitail said that the longer we are here, the more we will be able to see,' answered Zeeglit. 'For now, follow me and stay close so we don't get separated. What did you think of that, Zig?' And the other moogle answered without hesitation.

'That was the most exciting thing I've ever done – I could have kept going for ever!'

Zeeglit laughed and responded, 'I agree. That was how my father felt the first time and they couldn't get him off for a whole sunrise to sunset. He told me he went right round the whole thing three times and by the time he landed he couldn't walk straight!'

Chapter 12
Moon Spiders

Looking at the dimometer, Zeeglit began to walk off along what appeared to be a well-trodden path and he explained that there are many moogle traders who visit the moon-spiders every day to collect their threads to share with others.

'What do the moon-spiders get in return?' asked Zig, who understood that trade meant that something was given in exchange for something else: either goods or services.

'Ah, well, yes; I was going to mention that,' replied Zeeglit, somewhat sheepishly.

Alerted by his hesitation, Zig became suspicious. 'What do they want in return, Zeeglit?'

'Well, it's not much to ask really. What do you think they use to make their threads from?' he asked.

'I hadn't thought about it. Wait a minute; you're not telling me they use our fur, are you?' Now whilst Zig was very keen to help, he was also rather vain and the thought of returning home bald horrified him.

'They don't want all of it. They trade fairly but in return for the amount of rope we need they will expect quite a lot of hair. Ressa told me they are expert at plucking it and will take an even amount from all over so your coat will be considerably thinner but you will have no bald patches and it will soon grow back.'

Not at all happy at what he had just learnt, Zig walked in silence for a way and Gib, sensing his unease, offered to give up all his fur and then walked quietly beside him. Sounds from up ahead stirred Zig's natural curiosity and he became interested in what they were about to see.

From out of the gloom, their eyes began to pick out activity. They walked past small groups of moogles who were sat around and Zig was keen to see what they were up to. The first few seemed to be chatting and sharing food but as they moved deeper into the area of activity the scene changed. Here, moogles lay on the ground with legs and arms spread out.

'What are they doing? What can I see?' asked Gib.

They looked more closely and they saw: running all over the bodies of the moogles, in and out of their fur, were hundreds of tiny white spiders, each the size of a raindrop! On closer inspection, they could see rows of the tiny insects leaving their target carrying several strands of soft yet wiry hair and Zig felt a shudder of revulsion go through him.

'Oh no – I can't do that. I'm sorry, I just can't!' he said with feeling but Zeeglit said nothing, just continued weaving his way through the hive of activity and Zig had no choice but to follow with Gib scurrying to keep up.

Moogles of all shapes and sizes crowded round stalls displaying threads of every thickness from fine strands for waistcoats and tunics to thick rope of the size they were looking for. The stalls were lit with the familiar glow-lamps in a vast array of colours, making the scene look like a festival and there was a happy buzz in the air. Everywhere he looked,

Zig could see moogles choosing threads, rope and clothing. He would have liked to have stopped to take it all in but still Zeeglit continued and it appeared that he knew exactly where he was heading.

As the crowds began to thin, Zig was able to see what was in front of them and the sight almost took his breath away. Under the light of a full moon, thousands upon thousands of tiny moon-spiders were hard at work. Able to spin long, long lengths of thread, they worked their trade between the moon and back, creating a lacy web of carefully woven strands which appeared alive with activity as the tiny insects scurried up and down.

'Once a strand is completed,' Zeeglit explained, 'It is cut off at the top end and falls onto the floss where it is gathered and sorted. The finest threads and those which are the palest colours are set aside for clothing as they can be woven and dyed to make beautiful fabrics. The rest are taken to the processing area where they are twisted into different thicknesses from twine to the thickest rope.'

'Who does the sorting and processing?' asked Gib. 'That cannot be the spiders, surely.'

'No.' Zeeglit laughed. 'Once the thread has been woven and dropped to the clouds, it would be too heavy for the insects to move. The next stages are carried out by a hard-working team of moogles who live and work at the North Pole and never leave. They are organised by a wise and very fair supervisor called Glanteen and it is him that we are going to see now.'

Leading the way, he set off again and led them towards a raised clump of floss with steps cut into it. Up to the top they climbed, glow-lamps lighting their way. The mound was only about five metres high with a flat top and in its centre was a large cushion of floss with an elderly moogle sitting in comfort, surrounded by traders. As the little group approached, he looked up and his face broke into a smile and he stood up.

'It has been a long time but I would know the son of my old friend anywhere!' he greeted Zeeglit and those nearest to the supervisor moved back to allow the newcomers to pass.

'I hope we're not intruding but my father would have been sad if I was in the area and hadn't looked you up. I am Zeeglit. How are you keeping?'

'I am well, and Ressa?'

'He is well and will be sad not to have seen you.'

'Things here carry on as always and trade has never been better. You have come at a good time for today is a special day. It is the centre of our months of darkness and tonight there is to be a celebration. This is why there are more visitors than usual here today. You must join my party for the feast. But come: tell me why you are here and who you have with you.'

The group sat down with Glanteen and the introductions were made. It was obvious that he was fascinated by Gib and, in particular, his fur and, as he also didn't fancy having his fur plucked, he tried to hide behind Zig. Zeeglit explained why they were there and they discussed the grade of rope necessary for such a mission.

The conversation continued and, after a while, Zig and Gib wandered off to look at the view from the edge of the mound. Although there was no daylight, the full moon made it possible to see and they realised what a hive of industry this was. They watched teams of moogles sorting and gathering the completed threads and then dragging them off to the left. Moving around the edge to follow their progress, they saw them add the threads to piles already started. Many more workers were selecting threads from these stacks and taking them to others who were twisting them into thicker strands.

Following the production around the base of the mound, they saw the finished products being given to others who dragged them to one of the many colourful stalls for selection by the traders. They could see the traders still milling about, making their way from one stall to another, looking for a certain length or thickness of thread and carrying large coils of their wares around their shoulders.

Following a shout from, Zeeglit, they made their way back towards the centre.

'We will go and have a look for some rope that will do the job and Glanteen has kindly agreed to ask his workers to weave it into a net. However, there is just one tiny difficulty – he's very keen to obtain a bit of Gib's black fur. He has never seen anything like it before and says he would willingly trade it for the weaving. How do you feel about that?' he asked Gib.

'Oh dear, oh dear! Maybe I should not have come. This is not good.'

'I can tell you that my father says it doesn't hurt; it only tickles slightly, and we really do need the net,' coaxed Zeeglit.

'Well, I suppose it will have to be,' Gib agreed but Zig could see that he really wasn't happy about it.

'How about you Zig? Are you up for it?' asked Zeeglit.

'Do I have a choice?' he asked.

'Of course you do – but no fur means no rope,' was the answer and Zig knew he would have no choice, though the thought of having hundreds of tiny spiders crawling through his fur really gave him the creeps. 'Anyway, we will make our final choice of rope tomorrow and for now we have been invited to Glanteen's burrow to rest until the festivities begin: it will be a late night tonight!'

Following instructions, Zeeglit took them to a low, curved overhang marking the entrance to a tunnel and shouted, 'Hi-lo, anyone home?'

'Come on down,' came the response so they made their way inside. Lit by a procession of yellow and blue lamps, the corridor took on a mellow green glow and led into a large living chamber with more of the same colouring.

Relaxing in the sunken area was an extended family of several generations. Glanteen introduced them to everyone (though there were far too many to remember) and told them to make themselves at home. Zeeglit sat by his father's old friend and they were soon deep in conversation as Glanteen wanted to know all about Ressa. Zeeglit was fascinated to learn about the activities at the Pole but Zig made his way across the pod to watch two young males of a similar age to himself.

They were playing a game of Rentis which was one of the favourites played at home with his brothers. It involved placing twenty small pebbles in a circle and a stick in the centre with one end sharpened to a point. One player begins by spinning the stick and hoping it will end up pointing exactly to one of the pebbles. If it does, they take that pebble and spin again; if not, the turn moves to their opponent. The winner is the player with most pebbles when all have been taken.

'Hi-lo. May I join you?' he asked.

'Of course. Sit down and you can play the winner.'

So Zig sat and watched as the two played, noting that the taller of the two was definitely the more competent player. Sure enough, he was the winner and Zig was able to enjoy a good game against a worthy opponent. Although it was close, Zig was also defeated but it had been fun and he felt to have made a couple of good friends at the end of it. All the time the game continued, Gib sat quietly by, not uttering a single question and Zig was quite worried about him. Taking him to one side, he asked.

'Are you alright? You are unusually quiet this evening.'

'I am thinking too much.'

'What do you mean? What are you thinking about?'

'Now it is you who are asking all the questions!' Gib joked. But on a more serious note, he added, 'I am thinking that I do not like spiders. I have seen such creatures in other places and I have not liked them there either. I do not like their nasty little legs and I do not like to think of them running about in my fur. Yet I know this is something I must do.'

'I know how you feel,' Zig responded with feeling. 'I am also dreading the plucking. However, I do trust Zeeglit and if he says it is fine then I guess it must be. Would it help if I promise to watch over you when it's your turn and then you can do the same for me?'

'Would you do that for me? It would help me a lot. Thank you, friend.'

Just then, Glanteen stood up. 'The time has come. We must join the others to celebrate.'

Everyone filed down the passageway, joking and laughing and the newcomers were swept along with the jolly band. Outside, the party was in full swing. Musicians were playing a lively tune in the centre of the gathering and a handful of the younger traders and workers were dancing wildly. The lanterns had been arranged to create patches of different coloured lights and Zig and Gib were pleased to see that not a single moon-spider was in sight.

To one side of the dancers, a table had been laden with foods of many types: some of which were familiar but some of which neither Zeeglit nor Zig had ever seen before. It appeared that Glanteen and all the workers had provided the feast and everyone was welcome to enjoy their fill. Traders mingled with workers, old with young, strangers with friends and the night passed in a whirl of eating, dancing and laughter.

It was the early hours of the morning before the party began to break up and Zeeglit and Zig felt they should get some rest. They were just making their way back to Glanteen's home as he had insisted they must spend the night, when something caught Zeeglit's eye. Grabbing Zig by the arm he began to hurry him towards the darker area away from the glow-lamps and Gib hurried along behind.

'Where are we going?' asked Zig, sensing his friend's excitement.

'I think we are about to get one of the most spectacular shows nature has to offer!' he answered mysteriously.

Sure enough, a few seconds later, the most spectacular display lit up the sky before them. Shifting, swirling lights in the most amazing array of colours danced before them and the three friends stood mesmerised.

'What is it?' Zig asked breathlessly.

'I believe this is called the Northern Lights,' answered Zeeglit. 'It is something that you will only ever see near the North Pole and even here it is not often seen. Ressa saw it once, many years ago, and I've always wanted to. Isn't it amazing?'

'It certainly is.'

'I have never seen this before,' said Gib. 'I think I will also remember this for a long time.'

The three creatures forgot how tired they were and sat down on the floss to enjoy the most amazing light show of their lives. Fingers of blue and purple feathered across in front of the translucent moon chased by shadows of turquoise and gold. Glowing green ghosts danced and spiralled across a contrasting purple background and swirls of pink, whipped by the Polar winds, joined in the performance. It was only when the last snakes of iridescent green light finally slithered away over the horizon that they stood and retraced their steps in silence, each reluctant to break the spell of what they had just witnessed.

When they reached the burrow, the visitors were shown to a guest pod. It took no time at all for them to fall sound asleep on their comfortable beds of catilly floss: both moogles dreaming about the sight they had just seen though Gib was later to report that he'd had a very poor night's sleep because of nightmares involving large white spiders!

It seemed no time at all before they were woken by Glanteen as he made his way to start his day's work. He suggested they have a look around the stalls and select the rope that would suit their purpose and then he would arrange to have it taken to be made into a large net to carry the star.

After a quick roll in the dew and a brief grooming session they set of to see what they could find, having all agreed they had eaten so much last night they would probably not want anything at all that day. Making their way past several stalls they came to one that they had noticed the previous evening. The rope looked strong and there looked to be plenty of it. They then went back to the mound to report their findings to Glanteen and the process of making a net began.

However, this also meant that the time had come for the travellers to donate some of their fur and it was with great trepidation that they followed one of the workers to the area where they had seen the moon-spiders at work when they had arrived yesterday. Zeeglit was not feeling so confident now that the time was here but putting on a brave face, he suggested that he go first to reassure the other two that there was really nothing to be worried about and, removing his waistcoat, he took his place on the floor as directed.

Once he had made himself comfortable, one of the workers gave a command and hundreds of tiny white spiders made their way onto his body. Swiftly, they moved over and under his fur, taking strands from everywhere and ferrying them away, to be quickly replaced by others doing the same. The whole process took about half an hour of our time and despite the fact that Zeeglit was obviously in no distress, neither Zig nor Gib was any happier about the idea.

Once Zeeglit had stood up and they had reassured themselves that he had no bald patches, it was time for one of them to take their turn. As they argued over which one of them should go first, the decision was suddenly taken out of their hands as an experienced worker, sensing their reluctance and having experienced this before, suddenly picked Gib up and plonked him down on his back, shouting for the spiders before he had a chance to escape.

As he had promised, Zig stayed close by and shouted encouragement to the terrified creature as the spiders set about their business. With his eyes tight shut, Gib whimpered and tried to stay still as the scurrying feet tickled his body and the plucking prickled his skin. Being so small, the process did not take as long as it did for a moogle but the spiders had been rather greedy when they sampled the soft, black fur; the like of which they had not seen before. As he stood up, Zig was shocked to see how thin the little creature's fur looked and was angry that they had taken advantage of him in that way.

Zeeglit also looked shocked and he demanded a nearby worker provide Gib with a small waistcoat as compensation. As this was being found, it was Zig's turn and he was even more unhappy about losing some of his rich, glossy coat than he had been before. However, he allowed himself to be led to the appropriate place and lay down to await his fate.

Spreading his arms and legs wide as he had seen the others do, he closed his eyes tightly and heard the worker shout the command. And then he felt them: thousands of tiny feet passing across his skin. Whilst not exactly painful, he could feel the strands of his fur being pulled out and Zig realised that he liked this even less than he thought he would. He was aware of Gib calling reassurance (very brave considering what had just happened to him) and he tried to think through the events of the previous night's celebrations to take his mind off what was happening.

Eventually it was over and Zig was allowed to get up. Feeling slightly sore, he ran his hands over his fur. There was still an even coverage but it was certainly a lot thinner than it had been when he woke up that day. Looking at Gib, he noticed that he was now looking rather smart in a bright red waistcoat and it made him smile for the first time that day.

'All over with now,' said Zeeglit. 'It will grow back very quickly. Now, I was thinking: what if we take some extra rope to use to rescue the prisoners in the sapphire mines. I have had an idea how it might be done.'

As they walked back to the mound where Glanteen could be found, he went on to explain his plan and Zig felt it was worth a try and that they should take more rope if possible but not if it meant having to be plucked again. However, when Zeeglit told his old friend about the rough treatment that Gib had received, he was very sorry and had no problem granting them extra rope for their trouble. The net was also delivered to the mound shortly after they got back there and they were very pleased to see it looked exactly as they hoped it would.

Now, although the rope woven from the moon-spiders' threads is strong, it is also lightweight, making it possible for the traders to carry a good quantity with them as they travel. So it was that the moogles had no difficulty in lifting the bundles they needed to take with them. Once they had said their thanks and goodbyes to their host, they agreed that Zig should carry the larger bundle of the net whilst Zeeglit could manage the slightly smaller bundle containing rope for their second plan. Making sure the packs were securely attached to each other's backs, they set off back from the Pole in the direction they had entered the day before.

For some reason, it was only then that Zig remembered something that Zeeglit had said before they had left the fallen star: 'Getting back will be more difficult.'

'Zeeglit, how are we to get back to the star? You said we can't travel back the other way on the Jet Stream, so how do we get home?' he asked.

'There is a way that we can use but it is not without some element of danger,' he replied. 'We are heading towards the Polar Ramp at the moment. I asked Glanteen the way before we left.'

'What is that? What is a ramp?' joined in Gib. 'Will I like it? What will I see?'

Pleased to see that the little space traveller seemed to be recovering from his ordeal with the moon-spiders, Zeeglit continued, 'My father says the ramp is like a huge ice slide. We just have to climb to the top and slide down the other side.'

'That sounds a bit tiring but not too hazardous. Where does the element of danger come into it?' asked Zig.

'Ah, well,' said Zeeglit, casually, 'It comes as we shoot off the bottom of the slide and sail across the Jet Stream before hopefully landing in a clump of soft floss on the other side.'

'What!' exclaimed Zig.

'Oh dear! Oh no! I may not live much longer. What can I do? What will I see?' gibbered Gib.

'Worry not, my friends. I'm sure we'll be fine.'

'Don't you mean, "we *will* be fine"?' asked Zig, but Zeeglit had turned and was striding out and they had to hurry to keep up with him.

Darker, now they were away from the lights of the trading post and not benefitting from the full moon of night time, they had to tread carefully and Zeeglit used his gantate to add a little light. Once they had passed the area where they'd landed the day before, he used his dimometer to find the area he was searching for and it wasn't too long before they saw the land before them begin to rise upwards.

Not able to see more than a few metres in front of their faces, the climb was slow and also tiring as the slope became steeper, the higher they climbed.

'Steady now,' said Zeeglit. 'We must be nearly there.' And he dropped to all fours and inched his way on up.

'This is it!' he announced suddenly.

Joining him on the edge, Zig and Gib couldn't get a true idea of the height they had climbed as the ground dropped away in front of them but they could see hardly any distance ahead.

'We can't get on that!' exclaimed Zig. 'It would be suicide – there's no way we can see where we would be going!'

'I know it looks tricky,' agreed Zeeglit, 'but it is the only way back unless you want to travel right around the world and many moogles use this route every day and land quite safely.'

He spoke with a confidence he was far from feeling but just as he finished speaking, the little group of three were joined unexpectedly by a trader who was laden down with a large bundle of threads.

'Hi-lo, stranger,' Zeeglit greeted him. 'Have you travelled this way before?'

'All the time,' was the reply. 'There's nothing to it.' And before they had time to ask him anything else, he heaved himself and his wares over the edge and sitting on the pack, he disappeared into the darkness below. Listening carefully, they heard nothing else and had to assume he had reached the other side.

'Ready?' asked Zeeglit.

'As I'll ever be!' answered Zig.

'We'll go together so we end up in the same spot,' Zeeglit announced. 'If Gib hangs on to you and you sit on your pack, I will jump straight on behind you as you go.'

So that is what they did. On the command: 'Ready, go!' Zig, with Gib clinging tightly round his neck, scrambled over the edge and just had time to get his pack underneath him before he began to slide. Almost immediately, he felt Zeeglit land behind him and took comfort from the closeness of his friend.

They slid faster and faster and, as they descended, so the skies got lighter as they moved away from the Polar region and the scene below them came into view. His heart in his throat, Zig saw the great void racing towards him at an alarming rate as they hurtled down the icy slide. Faster and faster they went, the wind whipping through their recently thinned fur, chilling their blood and making their teeth chatter.

Just before the end, the slide levelled off and all three creatures let out an involuntary scream as they shot off the end of the cliff and sailed over the channel of the Jet Stream. Looking down, they could see sailing ships of floss racing round the invisible track, some loaded with passengers, some not. Looking ahead at the rapidly approaching floss they had no time to inspect their landing strip before they were plonked unceremoniously into an area of Alto-tuft bushes.

Thankful for the protection they offered, Zeeglit pulled himself out from the shrubbery and looked around for the other two. Zig was not hard to find, having landed close by and, after checking that he was not hurt, he turned to look for Gib. This was not so easy and it was a good few minutes before they found him; looking very sorry for himself, with his new waistcoat caught on a particularly high branch.

After helping him down and assuring him that his waistcoat had not suffered, they decided they would travel a safe distance away from the edge of the cliffs before settling down for the night. Zeeglit checked his dimometer for the best route whilst Zig picked a few handfuls of the newest shoots from the bushes for an evening meal.

Exhausted from the events of the day and the shortage of sleep the previous night, they made slow progress and when they spotted the first suitable bank of soft floss, they were all keen to stop. It didn't take long for the two moogles to scoop out a shallow burrow and they huddled together inside to warm up as they enjoyed their food and recalled events from the last two days. They then decided to take advantage of an early night so they could be up and off bright and early the next day.

Gib was the first to wake the following morning, excited to see if his friends had arrived and he danced about impatiently as the moogles enjoyed their morning grooming routine. As the first fingers of morning sunlight began to creep across the floss towards them, they set off towards the glums and their hidden treasure.

Chapter 13
Visitors from Outer Space

Sure enough, as they came within sight of the glums, things looked exactly as they had a couple of days previously. There was no sign of any intergalactic visitors or, indeed, any tracks to indicate there had been visitors of any kind. They made their way so they were overlooking the scene and close enough to the circle to be ready for the expected arrivals.

'Are you sure your friends will come?' asked Zig.

'I called them, so they will come. We must wait. I listen.' And he sat down with his eyes raised upwards, head tilted to one side and, for once, he was silent.

Not sure how long they would have to wait, Zeeglit and Zig made themselves comfortable nearby and talked about families, friends and experiences, each simply taking pleasure in the others company and being alive.

Half way through the morning, Gib suddenly jumped to his feet. 'They are coming!'

Zeeglit and Zig stood too; both curious and excited to see what was coming; having no idea what to expect. At first they saw nothing but continued to look in the same direction as Gib and then they saw something. A cluster of transparent spheres reflecting shades of green and red shimmered towards them.

As they got closer, within each orb they could see a creature similar in appearance to Gib and Zeeglit counted ten of these bubbles.

Gib was now beside himself with excitement: jumping up and down and waving wildly with his arms to indicate a suitable place for them to land. The two moogles stood back and watched from a safe distance though Gib seemed to stand alarmingly close to the landing zone but they needn't have worried: making no sound at all, the small crafts, vibrating softly, set down gently all around where he was standing.

No sooner were they on the ground than the top of each sphere appeared to pop open and the travellers began to disembark. Similar in size to Gib, their fur varied in shade from jet black to a lighter grey and Zeeglit guessed that this was down to age. It was obvious that they all knew each other and they chattered excitedly. The newcomers appeared to speak as fast and continuously as Gib did, though what was actually being said was a mystery as they spoke in a language that the moogles could not understand. They guessed that he was trying to give them a brief rundown of the problem of the fallen star as he was pointing in that direction but they seemed more interested in the state of his fur (or lack of it) and the snazzy red waistcoat.

There appeared to be a definite leader of the group. One distinguished gibberwit with a covering of fine grey curls was asking most of the questions and it was to this individual that Gib seemed to direct his story. He kept glancing at the two moogles and Gib appeared to be explaining their part in his rescue and the last few days.

Feeling they'd given Gib enough time to become reunited with his friends, they moved forward towards the group. All eyes turned towards them and Gib introduced them in the language of the moogles:

'I am proud to introduce some of my people.' Indicating the obvious leader, he continued, 'This is Holsheed: one of the greatest adventurers that our people have known. He will be a great help in our efforts to replace the star.'

He then introduced Zig as his saviour and Zeeglit as a wise companion. Feeling he should say something, Zeeglit spoke slowly and clearly so that the adventurer could understand him:

'Hi-lo, and welcome to our land. We are so glad you were able to come. We have such a problem and Gib said you may be able to help us.'

Speaking surprisingly fluently, Holsheed answered, 'We are pleased to be here, friend. From what our brother has told us, you have indeed got a problem but one that does not just affect you. If the stars begin to fall out of place, the whole of your galaxy will become unbalanced and who knows what might happen.' Then turning towards Zig, he continued, 'I believe we have you to thank for your bravery in rescuing Giberaldasky. He will be forever in your service.'

'Thank you, but I don't want him to be. He has his own life to lead and places to go, things to see,' said Zig, feeling it was important to get this thing cleared up.

'Ah, no, it is our law that his life now belongs to you and he is honour bound to help you.' Then, turning back to Gib, he asked in the language that the moogles could understand, for a look at the star.

So, it was that the two moogles made their way back to the edge of the singed floss accompanied by the group of gibberwits. This time, Zeeglit did not bother to interrupt the gigantic groaning glums as he knew he would get no response so he carefully lifted back the top layer to reveal the small star laying at the bottom of the hole it had created. Zeeglit was alarmed to see how little the star now vibrated and he was sure it also looked duller than it had before.

As he moved back to allow the travellers to see, they all scrambled into the hole, swarming around the star, chattering constantly and examining every last angle. Waiting and watching the thorough investigation, Zeeglit was filled with hope that these small intergalactic travellers may be able to help as they seemed very serious in their intent and, after all, they had bothered to come!

After a full inspection, the full team of gibberwits climbed out of the hole and Holsheed suggested they move away from the overwhelming sound of moaning so they could discuss the situation. Moving back towards the landing site, they found a flattish area of floss where they could see the area well and sat in a group where everyone could listen to and take part in the planning.

Zeeglit began the discussions by explaining how and when the situation at home had changed and they estimated that the star must have fallen a good few months ago to have had the effect that it had. They all agreed that the star needed to be replaced in its original position and Holsheed assured the moogles that he knew exactly where it had come from. He also felt that the plan to raise the star using a large, strong net was a good one and he said that he knew of the work of the moon-spiders, having come across them somewhere in his past and that their rope was likely to be strong enough.

There was a break in the talks whilst Zig opened up the pack with the net that they had brought back and it was examined by a couple of the gibberwits who, he was told, were the best engineers and would know if the rope was up to the job. Luckily, the verdict was good and so the discussions moved on to deciding how the ropes could be attached to the space-craft and whether they would be able to take the weight.

Once again, there was a pause whilst the two engineers and a couple of helpers disappeared back into the hole with the star to estimate the weight and calculate the pressure on the net if it took the weight of the star. Again, the results were positive and it appeared that each space-bubble had a retractable hook underneath that could be lowered for lifting purposes and that they should be able to take the weight if eight craft were used which would leave two to act as guide and lookout.

Once the general plan had been established, Holsheed said that his pilots were in need of a break as they had been travelling for a long time to reach the Altostratus (they had set off as soon as they received the message from Gib) and they decided that it would do no harm to wait until the next day to try out their plan. This decided, they got what they needed from their ships and made their way back to the camp established the previous night.

For a while, the moogles sat talking to the very well-travelled gibberwits and learning about some of the more interesting places they had visited over the years. Gib also told them the story of their adventure to the North Pole and Zeeglit thought that it must be exhausting to live constantly with creatures that talked as much or as quickly as gibberwits, yet he also realised that he had become quite attached to their small friend in the red waistcoat.

Just before dusk, Zeeglit, aware that the gibberwits had arrived without food and must be hungry, suggested to Zig that they should go and gather some alto-tuft for a meal. Telling the others what they were going to do, they set off in the direction they had travelled the day before as they had seen several places where the shrubs were growing.

However, they had not gone far when they saw an unusual cloud structure just off the track to their right. (What you have to remember is that unlike on earth, the landscape on the clouds is constantly shifting: some things stay the same whilst others shift and move from place to place with the wind.) The crusty grey mass was formed like a huge tunnel and Zig laughed.

'Wow! That looks good. I didn't see that yesterday.'

Zeeglit was more hesitant. 'Neither did I.'

'Let's go that way. I'm sure we will be able to find some food on the other side.'

'I'm not sure. It looks clear enough but after the tower I think we should stay on this route.'

'Are you joking?' asked Zig. 'I can see right the way through and there's nothing inside there. It would be much more fun to go through.'

Zeeglit had to agree that it did look fun and he didn't want to appear dull so, though not really happy about the idea, he agreed to go through.

As they entered the tunnel, they could see nothing suspicious: the surface underfoot was solid and the way ahead clear. Zig found that he could make his voice echo so he spent the time making hooting sounds and amusing them both with the reverberation. Zeeglit relaxed and in no time, they had made it through to the other side.

It wasn't far the other side before they found a cluster of tuft bushes growing and both moogles picked a feast of tender shoots for the intergalactic visitors. Once they had gathered a fair amount, they turned back towards the camp. Chatting about the plans for the next day, they passed into the grey arch of the tunnel without a second thought but this time things were not so straight forward. When they reached the halfway point, there was a strange rumbling sound behind them and Zeeglit turned around.

'Run!' he shouted and, grabbing Zig's arm, he began to pull him along.

'What's the matter?' asked Zig, stopping to turn around and have a look. 'Oh my!'

Behind them, the tunnel was closing in: the roof was flowing down to meet the floor and it was gaining on them! Turning back to run, Zig lost his footing and fell, taking Zeeglit down with him. Landing close together, Zeeglit just had time to pull his waistcoat over their heads before the choking grey floss covered them and, after a few more moments, all was silent.

Finding they had enough air to breath for now was a relief to Zeeglit but he didn't know how long it was likely to last. Trying to keep calm, he asked.

'Are you hurt?'

'My arm,' came the strained answer. 'What about you?'

'I'm fine. Can you move?' asked Zeeglit.

'No. Not at all. I can't even lift my head. Can you?'

'Not much but I think I can reach your arm. I've never tried it before but I'd like to see if I have the power of healing like my father.'

'Please try,' replied Zig so Zeeglit wriggled his fingers and inched towards his friend's wrist.

Laying his palm over Zig's fur as he'd previously watched Ressa do, Zeeglit was just wondering what to do next when he felt a strange tingling sensation in his palm. Warmth began to creep through his hand and he just knew this must be what his father felt.

'Can you feel anything?' he asked Zig.

'I can. My arm feels to be glowing and the pain is easing. It's wonderful!'

A few minutes later Zeeglit felt the warmth ebb away and he knew the job must be done.

'I think that's it. We will have to wait and hope help will come. I'm sure Gib will soon realise that we have been gone for a long time. In the meantime, I think we should be careful not to talk too much as I'm not sure how much air there will be in here.'

'Thank you, friend. You have a wonderful gift. I was thinking the same thing,' agreed Zig.

And so the two moogles lay side by side with their faces protected from the suffocating grey mass by a thin fabric waistcoat. Time passed slowly but Zeeglit had plenty to think about and for the first time the words of the seer came to mind:

'Only the hands of a healer can vanquish these foes from afar.' And a tingle at the back of his neck made his fur stand on end.

They tried to call for help but the dense floss muffled the sound. They tried to wriggle forward but the weight of floss from above pressed them to the ground. They tried to sleep but were frightened of missing something.

'What was that?' asked Zig a while later.

'What?' said Zeeglit.

'Listen.'

'I can't hear anything.' Zeeglit strained his ears. 'Wait a moment: I heard something then … Yes, there is something.'

'Help! Over here!' shouted Zig.

Listening carefully, they could hear faint scratching, scuffling noises coming from somewhere in front of them. Then again, there was silence: whatever it was had not heard them.

Time passed slowly and eventually both of them fell asleep.

'Wake up!' said Zig. 'I can hear something. Listen'

Zeeglit was feeling quite muzzy from the effects of a deep sleep and not enough fresh air. Trying hard to focus, he thought he could just make out a faint sound.

'Help! Please help us!' shouted Zig again, though Zeeglit was alarmed at how feeble he sounded.

This time, however, the sound didn't stop: it seemed to get nearer.

Zeeglit joined in the call and then they heard a sound which was music to their ears: 'Worry not. I am nearly there. I have found you.'

'Gib! Over here. This way.' called Zig.

The floss before them began to part and there was their rescuer. Zeeglit had never been more pleased to see anyone.

'Oh, thank goodness! How did you find us?' he asked.

'I will explain later. Now to get you out of this: I must clear a space so please wait.' And with that, he disappeared.

Sounds of activity reached their ears yet for a while they could not see anything. Then their rescuer reappeared and began moving floss from around and above them. He must have made at least fifty journeys pushing material out of their path until he finally said.

'Right, you move now.'

Wriggling along on their bellies, they managed to follow a hollow passageway carved out by the tiny creature and Zig marvelled at the effort he had put in to free them. It was several metres to the edge of the collapsed tunnel and once outside they could see the huge mass of floss he had had to shift in order to free them.

The two moogles sat outside drinking great gulps of the sweet fresh air and each praising the day they had rescued the small gibberwit from the sink hole.

Zig turned towards the intergalactic traveller and took his hands. 'Thank you, my friend – now we are even!'

'Yes, thank you,' added Zeeglit. 'But how did you know where to find us?'

'You were gone a long time,' said Gib. 'I sat talking with my friends. I thought you must be having trouble finding the bushes. Then I saw that it was getting dark and I was worried. I walked a little way back up the path to see if I could see you but there was no sign so I got more worried. I thought about going back to get help but it was getting darker all the time and I thought I would carry on the way we went before to help you. I walked all the way to the first bushes but you were not there and then I knew there must be trouble.

I came back along the path, looking for any signs that you had passed that way. At first, I saw nothing then I noticed a large mound of floss where there had been none the day before. I looked more carefully and I saw your paw prints leading off the path and they stopped suddenly as the floss began to rise up so I started to dig. I don't know what I would have done if I had not heard you shout because I was just beginning to think nothing could be alive under there.'

'I don't think we would have been for much longer,' said Zeeglit. 'The pressure from above was too great for us to move and there was very little air left. I thought we'd had it!'

Together the group trudged back to the burrow to explain to the group what had happened and apologise for the lack of food but what they had been collected lay crushed beneath as mound of crusty grey floss and no one was in the mood to go and get more.

As it happened, no one minded. They were all glad to see the moogles back safely and decided that they had all had a very adventurous day and that they should get a good night's sleep and find food in the morning.

Zeeglit had a very troubled night. He managed to doze off quite quickly but woke in a panic, gasping for breath. Tossing and turning, he couldn't get comfy and for the first time since he had left home, he really wished he hadn't come. He missed his family greatly and had come very close to being lost to them forever. In the early hours of the morning, he carefully picked his way over the others and made his way outside.

It had turned into a beautiful night and the stars twinkled brightly in the heavens. Lying on his back on the damp floss, paws behind his head, he looked for a space where the fallen star might have come from but he couldn't see one. As the wispy clouds of the Cirrostratus drifted across his vision, he marvelled at the size of the universe and how lucky they were to have the visitors sleeping close by – creatures that he hadn't known existed until recently. He wondered what other beings were out there and, not for the first time, he wondered whether there might even be life on the Oodle Pool far below.

Catching a movement out of the corner of his eye, he turned his head to see Holsheed coming from the burrow to join him.

'Couldn't sleep?' asked Zeeglit.

'I often find it difficult on the first night in a new homeland. The air is very different and although we are adapted to be able to cope with this, it feels strange. What about you?'

'When I close my eyes, I am back under the choking floss and I needed a bit of fresh air to clear my head. Lying here reminds me how wonderful our universe is. You must have seen some fantastic sights. What is your home like?'

The traveller thought carefully then answered, 'Our home is many light years away from here and it is a very long time since we have been there. However, it is a small planet – very overcrowded and not rich in natural resources, which is why many of its inhabitants become travellers. We search the galaxies for another planet with suitable conditions for our species to inhabit where we will be welcome but we have not yet found the right one. We are a peaceful race and will not live where we are not wanted. As we travel, we enjoy the varied sights we see and try to help where we can.'

'Do you really think you will be able to help with our fallen star?' asked Zeeglit.

'I certainly think it's worth trying. We noticed there was a star missing from just inside your galaxy but we had no idea where it had gone. One star out of place can have far-reaching consequences and we are pleased to be able to help. You can be sure you will not be the only ones to be noticing the effects.'

'Do you mean there are creatures living in other places you have visited?'

'Of course!' responded Holsheed amazed. 'There are many, many species living in all sorts of settings throughout this universe and beyond.'

'How I would love to see some of the sights you have seen,' Zeeglit sighed. 'Though I am amazed to know there is so much life beyond here.'

For a while, the two strange companions lay in silence gazing into space, each lost in their own thoughts. Feeling much more relaxed by now, as the sky began to lighten, they agreed to make their way back inside and try to sleep for what remained of the night.

The morning was a little overcast and, while the moogles took their morning roll in the floss, they wondered if the rescue plan would be able to go ahead. The air was damp and visibility not very good but they could just make out the shape of the glums. Zig went to gather some tuft with five of the pilots, having promised Zeeglit that he would keep to the main path and it wasn't long before they were all able to sit down for a morning meal.

By the time they had finished eating, the sky had begun to clear and there seemed no reason to delay any longer. Taking the pack containing the net down to the crash site, Holsheed took command of the situation. After trying, unsuccessfully, to talk to the glums, he turned his attention to the fallen star.

Shouting commands, he organised his crew into an efficient workforce to clear the floss covering the star. Lying exposed at the bottom of the hole, it looked a very sad thing and Zeeglit was worried that it may never recover, even if it was replaced in the heavens. The net was taken from the pack and laid out on the floss to be carefully examined by the engineers whilst other gibberwits took a very close look around the star.

At length, they all sat around to compare notes. It appeared that the star was in a bad way but it was thought that rescue had come just in time and that it should make a full recovery back out in space. The engineers also thought that the rope net was strong enough for the task and the next job was to get the net underneath the star and the end ropes spread out around it on the floss ready to hook up to the space-ships.

This was rather more complicated as the gibberwits had to drag the net underneath the weight of the star, being careful that it did not get caught on anything or tangled up. Zeeglit and Zig helped to pull the support ropes but otherwise kept out of the way as the operation was being organised very smoothly without them.

At one point Zeeglit saw Zig and Gib deep in conversation and there seemed to be some sort of an argument going on. He was just about to go over and see what it was all about when Holsheed announced that they were ready and eight of the pilots all went to get their craft and it was forgotten.

It was a fantastic sight to see as the small, shimmering spheres slowly shook before lifting gracefully into the air and each making their way to land alongside one of the rope ends. Holsheed was one of the two visitors left and once he had supervised the landing of his fleet, he headed over to where the two moogles were standing.

'We are now ready for the last step before we leave. The ships will lift and hover a little way from the ground and lower their carrying hooks. My chief engineer will help me secure the ropes to the hooks and we will then have to leave straight away as they will be unable to set down again and hovering in one position for too long with that weight underneath is not easy.'

'It has been very good to meet you, my friends, and I thank you once again for rescuing "Gib". Our journey is long but we will have the star back in its correct place by the time your sun has risen and set five times. I am sure it will make a full recovery and I hope this solves your problem.'

'We have a lot to thank you for,' said Zeeglit. 'And if it wasn't for Gib, we would no longer be here. We wish you a safe and speedy journey.' Then, turning to Gib, he added, 'What now for you, my little friend?'

Gib looked at Zig before he answered and Zig nodded. 'I am to leave with my friends. I would have stayed forever alongside Zig as I know I owe him my life but he has assured me that we are now even. I will never forget the last few days or meeting you both but it is a long time since I have been with my people and I would like to spend some time with them.'

'I think that's a good plan,' said Zeeglit smiling. 'But how are you to travel? I'm sure there is no room for more than one in each of these ships.'

'Ah, you will see. I will keep the star company and make sure it is safe as we travel. Now, goodbye my friends; we must go.'

After a short but emotional goodbye, the gibberwits began the process of securing the star and the moogles stood by to watch. Each of the eight supporting space bubbles lifted a short distance off the ground and a hatch opened underneath to reveal a horizontal hook. This tilted ninety degrees so that the rope ends could then be tied firmly around each one.

Once this was done and double checked, the two remaining pilots waved and jumped into their own craft still standing a little way off. Gib climbed into the net and secured himself in the curve between two of the arms of the star.

Then it was over: at a signal from Holsheed, the eight supporting spheres lifted carefully into the air in unison and the last that Zeeglit saw of Gib was his tiny red waistcoat flapping wildly in the breeze as the star successfully started its journey home.

'So that's what you two were arguing about earlier,' said Zeeglit, turning to his young friend.

'Yes. I didn't want him to spend his whole life following me around and, whilst I will miss him in some ways, he did go on a bit!'

'He certainly did. Perhaps it was a good thing we had the problem with the tunnel yesterday: at least it gave him a chance to save you. Without that he would probably never have gone.'

Nodding in agreement, Zig asked, 'What next? Do you think we can make it home today? Oh, look!'

Turning around, Zeeglit saw what Zig had been referring to: slowly and without saying a word, the glums were trudging away from the scene; one behind the other, heads held down.

'I wonder where they go now?' asked Zig. 'I wonder where they call home?'

'I have no idea but I do think it's time to go to your home now and find out how your father is. I'm not sure what my father will have to say about our adventures but he will be pleased to hear about the star.' Consulting his dimometer, just to make sure, they turned and left the empty, gaping hole behind them.

Chapter 14
Families Working Together

They were back in Zig's neighbourhood before the sun had reached full height. Rushing into his burrow ahead of Zeeglit, Zig was pleased to find his family gathered in the central chamber with Raylee looking much better than when he had last seen him. Ressa jumped up to greet his son and Pagloo was obviously very relieved to have all her family back under the same roof.

Everyone was keen to know what had happened to the star and sitting around together, Zig explained what they had done. Bim and Doon looked very envious when he explained, with great excitement, about the ride on the Jet Stream and their subsequent return from the North Pole.

Zeeglit could feel Ressa tense beside him.

'I thought I told you to avoid any dangers and take no risks,' he said quietly.

'You told me all about the Jet Stream ride, Dad. You did it,' he replied.

'That was different. I was older.'

'Magitail told us all about your adventures and she said you weren't much older than me the first time you travelled that way.'

'Hmmph! That's not the point,' responded Ressa.

The listeners were also sad to have missed the sight of the gibberwits in their space-bubbles but they had not been idle since their return home.

It appeared that as soon as they were back and had checked their father was okay, they called a meeting of all the local moogles to explain what had happened and what they had learnt. Whilst they were relieved to learn that their offspring were still alive, they could not think how to get them back home: although more than fifty locals had attended, most were either elderly or too young to be much help as a rescue party. The meeting had broken up at length, with everyone going back home to try and think of a solution.

'We've had an idea,' said Zig excitedly. 'Well, Zeeglit has. Tell them.'

'Well, it's not a full rescue plan as yet but it has possibilities. Seeing all the ropes available at the Pole made me think about bringing some for a rescue mission. I thought we might be able to lower them through the air vents and the prisoners could climb out. It needs a lot of work before it would be a full plan but it's just a suggestion.'

'I think it is definitely worth thinking about – it's more than we've come up with so far,' said Bim thoughtfully.

Turning to Raylee, Zeeglit asked, 'How are you feeling now?'

'Thanks to your father, I'm so much better. So are the others he's treated and we hope to be fit enough to help in any rescue mission. We have planned to hold another meeting later today which gives us a bit of time to think your ideas through before we meet.'

Settling down to think carefully about what could be done, Zeeglit was amazed how at home he felt with this family he had only met just over a month before and he was pleased to be able to relax in comfort for a while after the recent adventures.

By the time the afternoon meeting came around, they had the basis of a possible rescue mission and were keen to share these ideas with the other locals, though it would also depend on how many able-bodied individuals would be available to take part.

The gathering took place in a central area amongst the burrows where the floss was smooth from many years of trampling as the locals criss-crossed the area and children played. As Zeeglit and his friends drew close, he could see familiar faces amongst the crowd from his previous visit and he was welcomed with much enthusiasm. He was pleased to see how well many of his father's patients looked and he was hopeful that many of them would be well enough to help in any attempt at a rescue.

Sitting to one side of the group were nine, strong looking younger moogles. As Zig went over to greet them, Bim explained that these were the family and friends of the moogles that his brother had been staying with when he had avoided capture. Doon had gone to tell them what had happened the day before and they had come to help.

When everyone had gathered, Bim began to speak and everyone was quiet. He started by introducing Zeeglit to those who hadn't met him and he then went on to ask what ideas there had been since they last met but there was not much except many offers from those willing to help: some realistic, some not.

Then Bim described the plan that they had begun to put together that afternoon and, as he listened to it, Zeeglit felt that it did have a chance. The first part of the plan was for the rescue party to have a good look around the site for hazards. They would then have to alert the moogles trapped inside that they were going to be rescued and ropes would be dropped down into the sapphire caves for them to climb up.

Although there were many flaws in this plan, the group felt that it had possibilities and they decided that they would meet again at first light to iron out the difficulties, having had the night to think it through.

As you can imagine, it was all the family talked about that evening as they sat around, although from time to time, Zeeglit did wonder how the gibberwits were getting on with *their* rescue mission.

Pagloo was not happy that all her family should go off again but she could see that they would need all the help they could get, and in the end it was agreed that she would also go with them. The main difficulty was how to let the captives working in the caverns, know about the rescue. At length, Bim suggested the idea that had been going around in Zeeglit's mind but he hadn't liked to say it:

'I think I should go back in. I know the routine and they won't expect me to come back. The guards won't recognise me and I can let everyone know what to expect.'

'I'll come with you,' seconded Doon. 'I can tell those dragging the carts whilst you tell the miners. Otherwise, they'll be down the corridors when the rescue takes place.'

It was obvious that their parents did not like the idea at all but Zeeglit could not see any way around it and he asked Ressa to lend Bim his dimometer so that he could find his way straight through the tunnels to the second cavern as the directions were stored in its memory from the previous visit. It was felt that an early night would be a good idea to prepare them for the following day and Zeeglit had no problem in falling asleep as soon as he had snuggled down.

Before he knew it, Bim was shaking him awake and the new day had begun. After their morning grooming, they made their way back to the meeting area and it wasn't long before everyone had gathered. Bim suggested the idea that they had discussed and it was agreed that this would be the basis of their plan and they should aim to leave in the late morning to give them time to have a scout around the area before nightfall.

That only left the question of who would be in the rescue party and, by the time the family retraced their steps to their burrow to eat a quick snack before departing; a group of twenty moogles had been selected. These included Zeeglit and Ressa, the whole of Raylee's family, the fit young friends of Zig and a few other able-bodied locals.

The rescue mission began on a calm, bright morning and the mood amongst the crowd striding from amongst the burrows was positive. Zeeglit was at the head of the crowd with Ressa, Raylee and his family, and he was using the dimometer to find the way back to the sapphire caverns. As they walked past the hollow left by the fallen star, Zeeglit told his father and friends about the adventure they had had only yesterday. Thankfully, there was no sign of the white tower on their journey today and they made good time, many eager to be reunited with family and friends. Though they kept a look-out for thordite warriors, there were none to be seen but, just to be on the safe side, they walked in silence once Zeeglit warned them that they were getting close.

As they neared the place where Zig and Zeeglit had hidden when they first found the caverns, they could see the thordite sentries still on duty. They decided to make it their base camp and, once they had all arrived, they separated into search groups as they had previously agreed. Ressa, Raylee, Pagloo and a few of the older moogles remained behind at the "base camp" and the others separated left and right to see what was around the perimeter of the area. Zeeglit taught Bim how to use the dimometer and they took a small group to try and find the air holes above the main caverns from where the rescue would happen.

One group, led by Doon, took the path that led off to the right of the entrance. They had gone a little way when they had heard thordite voices up ahead. Dropping to the ground, they made their way behind some bushes and saw two sentries guarding the exit that the moogles had been shown out of. For the moogles with Doon, this was their first sight of the enemy up-close and they did not like what they saw. Doon realised that they must have put guards at this entrance since they had used it: presumably in case they came back!

They then crept quietly on behind the shrubbery until the guards were out of sight and then re-joined the path. They saw nothing else unusual and were just about to turn back for the base camp when one of the group pointed out a noticeably darker area of floss a short way off. They decided it was worth investigating and wandered over to look.

The darker area they could see from the path was, in actual fact, the raised tip of a very dark area of floss that was slightly lower than the surrounding area. They were just about to cross the area for a closer look when Doon remembered what Zeeglit had told them about his rescue of the young thordite female.

'No, stop!' he shouted. 'I think this is their weapon store.'

Staying where they were, they took a good look at the area in front of them. Other than the colour, there was nothing to indicate that this was anything unusual; there was no sound and no movement.

'Surely there would be guards if it was something so important,' said one of the group.

'I suppose they know how sensitive the area is,' said Doon. 'From what Zeeglit said, if anyone walks on it, they are very likely to set off the weapons underneath. I don't think there's any way we can check it out but we will report back to the others. I wish we had that dimometer – then we could take a note of where it is exactly.'

'If it is their store, there must be some easy way for the thordites to reach their weapons in a hurry,' said another.

'That's a good thought,' said Doon. 'Can anyone see anything?'

Spreading out, they looked around the raised area of floss concealing the sapphire caverns. It was quite difficult as bru shrubs grew thickly and could be very spikey if brushed against the wrong way.

'Over here! I think I've found something,' said the youngest of the group; a young female of about ten years called Froo.

She was kneeling down next to a small entrance that wouldn't have been seen unless you were looking for it. As they gathered around, they realised that this was what they had been looking for. A steep tunnel led down from the entrance and efforts had been made to conceal it from the outside. As no obvious paths led around to this area, the thordites had presumably decided it did not need to be guarded.

Dusk was falling as the groups began to make their way back to compare notes. The group that had gone to the left of the entrance had very little to report – they had seen no thordite activity and nothing to indicate that there was anything out of the ordinary about the area. In contrast, the group that had gone to the right were able to provide a lot of useful information.

Bim said that his group had managed to find the air holes to the two main caverns and also to the row of openings letting air into the large rooms where the thordites had been seen relaxing. They had scouted round the rest of the area but had not found anything else of interest. They had heard sounds of activity coming from the working cavern but had not dared to lean over the edge in case they were seen and might give away the element of surprise. They had, however, inspected the area to see if it would support the weight of the moogles as they tried to pull up the captives if the rescue went to plan. Their decision was that it was ideal: the surface appeared strong, the lip of the hole appeared to be slightly raised and there was a flat area surrounding this where the rescuers could lie, hidden from view, until the time was right.

Talking in hushed tones, the moogles sat and talked through their ideas until they came up with a plan using all the knowledge they now had. Eventually it was decided: taking advantage of the darkness, Bim and Doon would creep into the mines during the dead of night. They had decided to go in via the tunnel near the weapons store that Doon's party had discovered earlier as it wasn't guarded and they felt it must lead directly to the main cavern for easy access to the weapons if they were under threat.

A small group of the older moogles would go as far as the entrance with then so that they could block the start of the tunnel as soon as Bim and Doon had entered. This did mean that there was no return for the two but it would slow down any thordites who came rushing down the tunnel for their weapons.

Once inside, Bim would use the dimometer to find the main sapphire hall and they would hide themselves there until the workforce arrived the next morning. They would then slip quietly into the working groups (Bim digging for the stones and Doon pulling the carts) and begin to pass the word that there was to be a rescue.

The rest of the rescue party would remain at base camp for all of that day and keep an eye on the comings and goings from the main entrance. The actual rescue would begin when the sun was at its highest the following day; by which time all the moogles inside the caverns should be prepared. The weak point of the plan was that the two groups would have no way to communicate once Bim and Doon had gone back underground but they would just have to trust that it was all going as planned.

Once the plan was clear in the minds of all the rescuers, they settled down to get a few hours' sleep, taking it in turns to keep a watch on the thordite sentries. Zig and Doon slept surprisingly well but Pagloo kept a watchful eye on her two sons and dreaded the time when they would go back inside the mine.

When that time came, she hugged each one before they made their way quietly from the sleeping group; accompanied only by Raylee, Ressa, Zeeglit and two others. Keeping low and moving quietly, they skirted the edge of the thordite camp and made their way along the path Doon had taken earlier. Using the watery light of the moon, they passed the side entrance, taking care not to wake the guard who had fallen asleep on duty and kept going.

Pointing out the position of the weapons store which was impossible to see in the dark, Doon led the way to the entrance he had seen earlier; pleased to see that it was still unattended. Looking down through the entrance, Raylee was very unhappy about his two sons heading off into the gloom but he could see no alternative and, as Doon pointed out, they had no need to rush as they had several hours until dawn and the small backlight in the dimometer would give some small glow in the pitch-black tunnel.

Wishing them all the best and begging them to stay safe, the small group watched them disappear down the steep underground tunnel and then began to look around for the prickliest bru shrubs they could find to push into the entrance of the tunnel to create a blockage. Once they felt satisfied that their efforts would slow down any warriors looking to make a quick exit, they made their way back to the others at base camp and reported that all was going to plan so far.

Chapter 15
Back into the Mine

Once the light from the moon was completely blocked by the twists and turns of the tunnel, Zig and Doon stood still for a few minutes until their eyes began to adjust to the darkness. As expected, there was a small glimmer of stored solar light from the dimometer and gradually they were able to make out their surroundings. The corridor they were standing in was actually quite wide once it was away from the entrance and the surface underfoot was sound.

Listening carefully, they could hear no sound coming from below and only faint scrabbling from above as the others began to push material into the tunnel.

'Are you ready, brother?' asked Bim.

'Yes, but go slow. They may have guards on duty and it would be such a waste if we ran into one before we reached the cavern. I really don't want to see Isilit again: I wouldn't fancy our chances a second time!'

'I agree. We'll take it slow. Keep close to me and look for dangers. I'll follow the dimometer.' And so the two brave moogles began to make their way towards what they hoped was the central sapphire mine.

Luckily, the smooth surface and wide corridor made their progress relatively easy and no hidden thordites lurked in dark corners. Even though they had thought this to be a quick way out from the main mining chamber, they were still surprised how quickly they reached their destination. There was no sign of life at all and they were able to find a good hiding place fairly close to the work area so they would hopefully be able to slip into the crowd unnoticed as the workers arrived in the morning. Making themselves comfortable the two brothers chatted quietly to pass away the next few hours whilst making sure they did not fall asleep.

Once the first fingers of light began to walk down the wall opposite them, the moogles were able to have a good look around them. It appeared that work had been started on about four fifths of the walls and the surface lit by the light of the new day gleamed with blue fire. Water that had gathered in a lake at the base of the cavern was crystal clear and looked very deep. Bim could detect movement under the surface but couldn't get a clear look at what was making it.

'Look!' said Doon suddenly. 'They've blocked the way we left last time.'

Following where he was pointing, Bim could see bars fixed across the tunnel that led away from the far side of the chamber where Zeeglit had waited for them before.

'They've obviously tried to make sure they don't get caught out again,' he said. 'Let's hope we can get away with it!'

'Shhh,' whispered Doon. 'I can hear something.'

Sure enough, a few moments later, the first working party of the day arrived. A group of approximately thirty captives was led into the caverns by their guards. These five thordites were dressed in short, dark grey, belted tunics and from these belts hung their graplars. Barking instructions, they organised the workers into groups along the rock face and the day had begun.

Feeling they would be noticed if they went to join the workers straight away, Bim and Doon sat tight. Presently, the first of the moogles pulling carts began to arrive to take the gems away and then another group of workers was brought in. There was now quite a bit of hustle and bustle and the time had come.

Bim was the first to move: slipping in easily with the working party at the end of the line. Whilst he had a few surprised glances from his fellow workers, the thordites had not noticed his arrival and he was soon pulling out stones like the others.

Doon's task was not as easy as he did not have a cart to pull though he did know where they were kept; standing empty, waiting for the next worker to collect. Picking a moment when the guards were looking in other directions and a couple of workers with full carts were about to make their way down the tunnel, he made a dash to walk on the far side of one of the carts as it left the cavern. He knew that the carts were not watched in the tunnel as there was nowhere for anyone to go other than the conveyor belt where the gems were offloaded.

Once in that area, he stayed hidden alongside the cart as it was unloaded. Then, as it was pulled towards the tunnel again, he nipped alongside the wall to where the stationary carts were waiting. Picking up the rope of the first one in line, he made his way back to the cavern.

The moogles worked solidly for the morning until their backs felt as if they were breaking and their paws were raw from handling the rough stones. Taking a careful note of the position of the sun over the central air-hole, Bim noticed it was just before midday that the guards gave them the command to rest and all work stopped.

The workers made their way to where a cart, filled with tuft had been wheeled in and each took a handful before dropping gratefully to the ground near the edge of the lake to eat and ease their tired bones before the afternoon shift. Bim remembered how short these breaks had felt and, without drawing attention to himself, he began to talk to those around him about why he was there.

Doon, sitting with a different group was doing the same and was pleased to see how careful the others were to avoid making the guards suspicious. Whilst the majority of the group seemed excited, there were a few who were very sceptical and obviously felt there was no way out of their current situation.

All too soon, it was time to get back on their feet and begin again, but during the afternoon shift, Bim worked his way into another group and tried to spread the word around as many of the workers as he could.

Just as Doon was beginning to think he could do no more, the order was given to clear away and the shift had finished for the day. The moogles were led along a corridor and herded into a large, dark sleeping chamber. The smell was unpleasant: stale and heavy, there being no opening to admit fresh air. A large covering of mesh was rolled down across the opening and the moogles were secured for the night.

Giving the guards time to disappear up the corridor, the moogles that had heard whispers about a rescue, clamoured around Bim and Doon for more information. As quietly as they could, they made their audience sit and explained their plan. Those captives from the brothers' home area were amazed to see them back but were quick to reassure any doubters that Bim and Doon were genuine and not planted by the thordites to trick them.

When asked, Bim explained how they had managed to escape before and he was told about the extra security that had been put into place and how the guards had been very angry for the next few days. Doon went on to tell them about the carved images they had seen at the entrance to the great hall and about Isilit; their great leader.

'What do you want us to do?' asked a small, thin moogle, sitting in the corner. 'I don't think I could fight.'

'You won't have to,' answered Bim, reassuringly. 'If we are ready when the sun is overhead, we should be able to work together to drive the guards into the lake. I was watching today and I noticed that the light is quite blinding as it glances off all the crystals and the thordites won't be expecting anything to happen. We can use the element of surprise to catch them off guard and if we all move together, we should be able to back them into the water.'

'But what about the graplars?' asked another.

'We dodge them,' answered Doon. 'I know it sounds frightening but it will take them a few moments to get them ready and we will be watching for them.'

One rather muscular moogle made his way to where the youngsters were standing. 'I've been here for a long time and I think it's worth a try. I began to think I would never see my family again. Let me near them and I'll soon take their graplars off them!'

'Aye, me too,' came one passionate voice after another.

Before long, the atmosphere in the sleeping chamber had become charged with excitement and individuals who had been imprisoned for months or even years began to talk of home and family. A while later, Bim stood up again:

'My friends, I suggest we try to sleep. The morning will be with us soon enough and we will need our energy to climb the ropes.'

True enough, it seemed no time before the guards were at the entrance, lifting the mesh and shouting the commands that started the new day. No chance to freshen up, the workforce stood and shuffled out past the guard and down the corridor to start another day's work. Only today there was a sparkle in the downcast eyes of the moogles as they wondered about what was to come.

Taking their place alongside the others, Bim and Doon put their efforts into digging and ferrying the gems, keeping their heads down and making sure they didn't stand out from the crowd. Just like yesterday, the command to "rest" came shortly before midday and the workers queued up for their food. However, today no one seemed to have much appetite and eyes kept flicking towards the air-hole in the roof where the bright daylight filtered in.

Meanwhile, back at base camp, the rescue party had spent the first day watching the entrance to the mines but very little had happened. During the hours of darkness, they took turns to keep watch and Zig had taken a small group onto the mound to double check the route for the rescue. This was followed by a frustrating morning just waiting for the time when the rescue could begin and wondering what was happening underground, a short distance away. Zeeglit found himself picturing all those underground tunnels and hoping that Bim had mastered the use of the dimometer. Those watching the activity at the entrance had very little to report, other than a routine changing of the sentries on duty.

Finally, however, the time came to put their plan into action. It had been agreed that Pagloo, Froo and an elderly male, known as Blog, would remain at the base camp to keep an eye on the main entrance and then join the group as they made their escape. The rest were to take the ropes that Zeeglit had brought for the purpose and make their way to the opening over the main cavern: a route that had been marked out by Zig and his team the previous evening.

Moving carefully until they were out of sight of the guards at the entrance, the rescue squad made their way over the mound and were in position, lying on their fronts around the air-hole in groups of three well before the sun reached its height. Each group had a rope coiled carefully near the rim of the hole, ready to drop over the edge at the given signal and tied around the waist of the heaviest individual in each group. As midday neared, so one of the other two in the group held onto the rope ready to take the strain and those at the front lay poised; ready to throw the ropes over the edge.

Zeeglit had a different job: having edged his way right to the rim, he lay looking down into the cavern below; waiting for the moment when the sun would create the dazzling light display that would be the signal for the operation to begin. He could see the moogles sitting around, taking their rest but couldn't be sure which was Bim or Doon and had to just hope that everything was going according to plan.

Higher and higher, the sun crept and the walls of sapphire below began to dance with light. Then the moment was upon them.

'Now!' yelled Zeeglit as the sun reached its peak and beams of light bounced of each jewelled face and reflected in the deep crystal water below. Coils of rope snaked their way from above into the cavern and as if one, the moogles below stood and advanced towards them. As hoped for, the thordites were taken totally by surprise and those between the advancing moogles and the lake did not have time to reach for their graplars before finding themselves in the icy blue water.

Zeeglit, looking from his position above, watched the whole thing and saw the first moogles reach for the ropes and begin to climb upwards whilst the rescuers above took the strain. He also watched with concern as thordites from behind the workers took their weapons and began to advance. However, there were not so many of these and they were quickly overpowered by groups of determined moogles who took their weapons and flung them into the water, to be swiftly followed by their owners.

Before the first of the captives reached the rim of the hole, others were already on their way up the ropes and the rescue seemed to be going according to plan. The thordites in the water were in a bad way: they had obviously never learnt to swim (in fact, Zeeglit doubted they even used water to wash) and they were thrashing about like mad, trying to stay afloat. He was sad to see that there were some who had lost the battle to survive as moogles are very peaceful creatures but there was nothing that could be done. What was very worrying was the screams they were giving out as they might alert other thordites but, again, there was nothing they could do about that and he turned his attention to those climbing the ropes.

As groups of workers stood blinking in the bright daylight, they were quickly gathered into groups and led away towards the quiet side of the mound by other members of the rescue party. It had been agreed that they would all leave by that route so they could avoid being seen by sentries on guard at the entrances but that they would go in groups so that they could start moving away from the area as soon as possible. Once safely away from the area, they could split up and head towards their homes or stay together and make their way to Raylee's to rest if their journey was longer.

By now, more than half of the captives had reached the surface and Zeeglit could clearly see Bim and Doon helping the more reluctant climbers onto the ropes and it was clear that they were going to wait for the end. As yet, no more thordites had arrived in the cavern but he could see a small group of the tougher looking moogles waiting at the entrance to the tunnels with graplars held ready – yet one more thing he had never seen before!

As they came to the last few captives, it was clear that a few of them would be unable to climb the ropes and Bim began to tie the ropes around their waists for the rescuers to haul them up. This went well and Zeeglit was just thinking they had got away with it when he saw movement at the entrance to one of the tunnels.

Four thordite warriors came at a run and a fight broke out with the moogles who were ready for them. Thordites are larger and are an aggressive species, but the moogle captives had been held in dreadful conditions for a long time and had had enough. Though the weapons felt unfamiliar in their hands, they soon overpowered the warriors and Zeeglit looked away as they made sure they would not get in the way of the rescue.

Finally, the last of the moogles, including Bim and Doon were on the ropes and the lake below held the now lifeless bodies of many thordite overseers. Then, into the cavern came an army: a message must have been relayed to the warriors relaxing in the main chamber and they had come ready for battle. It appeared that the sight before them made them very angry indeed as their battle cries echoed around the cavern and chilled the blood of the moogles above.

Running forward, they jumped for the ropes and began to climb, hand over fist, gaining on the moogles ahead of them. However, the moogles had had a head start and as soon as they gained the solid rim of the air-hole, the rope was let loose and disappeared over the edge, taking the climbing warriors to a watery grave below.

'Run fast!' shouted Zeeglit as the last moogle was safe and they raced as fast as their short legs would carry them across the floss. He could image the rest of the thordites trying to make their way out to their weapons store at that very moment and he knew the bru shrubs, though very sharp, wouldn't hold them up for long.

'We must separate,' shouted Raylee. 'I'll go back for Pagloo and the others and you must each go in small groups and head in a different direction. We will meet up again at home. Luck be with you all!'

'We'll come with you, friend,' said Ressa and the three peeled away from the others and made their way back towards the base camp. This time there appeared to be no-one on guard at the main entrance and no thordite activity could be seen at all. Hurrying across to where they had last seen Pagloo they were surprised to see the area was empty. Thinking they were hiding somewhere near, Raylee called.

'Pagloo! Pagloo! Come quickly! We must hurry.'

The silence that greeted them was deafening.

Raylee called again and this time Ressa joined in. A slight movement from behind a nearby shrub caught Zeeglit's eye and hurrying over, he found Blog, badly injured but alive. As the older moogles joined them, he tried to speak.

'It was so quick. We could do nothing. She took them.'

'Who took them? Where?' asked Raylee, anxiously.

'She was one of them but very grand. Long, blue gown. With guards.'

'Which way did they go?'

Pointing out across the floss, he added, 'They didn't walk.'

'What do you mean?' asked Ressa.

'They had a machine. It glided above the ground.'

Looking in the direction Blog had pointed, Zeeglit could see that the surface of the floss had been disturbed and quite a clear trail led off into the distance.

'We can follow them,' he told Raylee. 'Let's go now so that we don't lose the tracks.'

'Not so fast,' interrupted Ressa. 'I don't want you in danger again. This night's work has been enough and I hate to think what your mother would say if she knew what you've been up to. You need to go back to the settlement and alert the others then you can wait there for me.'

'No. That's not fair. I've come this far and I can help. I've spoken to the thordites and I know what Isilit looks like.'

'He has a point,' added Raylee. 'I can see why you wouldn't like it, Ressa, but if he's with us we can keep an eye on him.'

Reluctantly, Ressa agreed and Raylee turned to Blog. 'Do you think you can make your way back home to let the others know where we have gone?'

'I'll do my best,' was the reply.

'Take care. There may be thordite warriors anywhere.'

With that, Blog began to limp off in the direction they had come the day before and Zeeglit turned towards the tracks with Ressa and Raylee and began to stride off in the direction they led.

Chapter 16
Into the Thorite's Homeland

Zig had been very relieved to be reunited with Bim and Doon as they came out of the cavern and when the groups went their separate ways, they had stuck together. Joined by half a dozen others, including four of those who had attacked the thordite warriors, they made their way as quickly as they could across the mound of the caverns in the direction they had escaped previously.

There was no planning behind this: they were just following Raylee's instruction to separate; but it did bring them down very close to the side exit they had used for their escape. No thordites could be seen as they approached but they were anxious to get away as fast as they could and they started to run as soon as they were on the flat. However, they hadn't gone far when a shout went up:

'Over there! Running away – get them!'

Looking around, Doon didn't like the sight that met his eyes: The army of warriors that had entered the cavern last had made their way past the blockage in the tunnel and had helped themselves to a selection of weapons from their store. They were now grouping a short distance from the armoury and preparing to launch their attack.

'Faster! They've got to their weapons store!' yelled Doon but the legs of a moogle are not very long and there is a limit to how fast they can go.

Seconds later, an almighty flash lit up the floss around them and a thunderbolt smashed into the ground just to their left. Another flash and this time the explosion was just behind them.

'Zig-zag!' shouted Zig and they began to weave left and right as they ran to confuse the warriors. Another thunderbolt cracked close by but the moogles didn't have time to be terrified. On they ran, ducking and diving and trying to stay on their feet whilst the one-sided battle raged around them.

Now one thing that happens to the stratus if it is attacked in this manner is that it begins to break up and this was what happened now. As each thunderbolt struck the surface, cracks began to appear and sections of the clouds separated and began to drift apart.

'Stay close!' shouted Zig as he realised what was happening but it was already too late: one by one, the moogles found themselves on separate little floating islands, drifting in the same general direction but becoming further apart.

A thordite is not able to move far from their weapon store when they are in a battle as each lightening shaft and thunderbolt is launched separately and they are too heavy to carry far. As the distance between the moogles and their attackers grew, the brothers became more relieved yet more aware of the new danger they now faced.

Zig and Bim were quite close and were just wondering if there was anything they could do to steer their islands when one of the others in the group found the answer. Bringing his chunk of floss to rest between theirs, he showed them how he had guided his craft by lying with one arm or the other hanging over the side to act as a rudder. Quickly, shouting to attract the attention of the others, they explained what needed to be done and gradually, most of the sections were joined back together.

Sadly, a couple moogles were too far away but at least they were moving away from the thordites and would eventually come to rest against some area of floss, from where they could make their way home. Luckily, Doon was one of those who managed to join with the group and it wasn't long before they came to a solid mass of floss where they could safely continue their journey.

Feeling very relieved to have escaped from the caverns as well as the thordite attack, they made a very merry band as they neared the settlement. They had talked in length about the rescue as they walked along and had decided that the rest of the groups should have been able to escape in safety if the attack had been against them as no other groups had left in the same direction.

The first stars had just become visible as they rounded the last corner and they looked forward to a great party that night. However, as they got closer, they were surprised to see groups of moogles sitting around, talking in quiet voices or sleeping and there wasn't the sense of celebration they were expecting. Wondering what had happened, they were just about to make their way into their burrow when a neighbour stopped them.

'You won't find anyone at home,' he began. 'Come and sit with us and Blog will tell you what he can.'

Feeling very worried now, they followed their friend to the entrance to his burrow where a group of moogles sat around Blog who looked as if he had taken quite a beating.

'What happened?' asked Bim, as the brothers took their place amongst the group.

'I'm so sorry. There was nothing I could do,' began Blog. 'They have taken your mother and Froo. Raylee, Ressa and Zeeglit have gone to try and find them.'

'Who took them?' asked Zig, alarmed.

'Zeeglit said he thinks she is the ruler of the thordites and he had seen her before. She wore long blue robes and was riding in a machine.'

'Isilit!' gasped Zig. 'She hates moogles.'

'What do you mean by "a machine"?' asked Bim.

Blog described the creation that had glided off into the distance carrying Pagloo and Froo:

'It was like nothing I have ever seen or even imagined,' he began. 'The body of the machine was made from some sort of transparent crystal and it shone in the sunlight. It was carved to have a high back, flat underside and a curved front that came up in front of the riders. There were no sides to it and I could clearly see two bench seats. She sat on one and two thordite warriors sat on the second, slightly higher seat behind her. She made your mother and Froo sit at her feet.'

'How did it move?' asked Bim. 'Were there thordites to pull it?'

'Oh no,' Blog replied. 'That was what was so amazing. One of the thordites had some sort of control leaver and the carriage rose up off the ground, hovered for a moment and then set off above the surface at a speed faster than a moogle could travel.'

'How did our father know which way to go after them?' asked Doon.

'The machine left tracks in the floss,' replied Blog.

Doon jumped to his feet. 'Coming then?' he asked his brothers.

Zig was ready to follow but Bim suggested they needed time to get some sort of plan together and he persuaded his brothers to rest and eat whilst they decided what the best action would be.

Neighbours provided tuft for the group as they talked about what should be done and about the machine that Blog had described. Bim said that it must be using the gas they had extracted from the sapphires and he reminded the others about the pictures they had seen carved into the great arch in the caverns and the extra lift they had experienced when they jumped in the caverns.

By the time they were ready to leave, there was a group of twenty moogles ready to help. Bim, Doon and Zig were joined by several of their neighbours and a handful of the moogles rescued from the mines, including the group that had escaped from the thordite fire-bolts.

They had decided to make their way back to the base camp; take a look at the tracks and then rest until morning as they would be unlikely to follow the tracks in the dark and they needed some sleep to be refreshed for whatever faced them the following day.

This was what they did and by first light the next day, they were heading off across the stratus following a trail of grey, disturbed floss. A couple of times, they thought they could make out moogle footprints but they couldn't be sure they belonged to their friends.

They allowed themselves a short rest at midday and most sat quietly, thinking about the events of yesterday and wondering what else lay in store. Although no one said it, they wondered what the chances were of rescuing Pagloo and Froo and where the three other moogles were at that moment.

Thankfully, only a little wind blew that day and the tracks remained clear. They were aware that the floss was becoming darker and they were entering an area where moogles generally don't travel for fear of meeting thordites. Trudging on, they began to think they were going to have to make camp for a second night before they found anything, when Zig heard noises up ahead and they decided to move a little way off the path and hide behind a dense thicket of shrubs whilst a few went ahead to see what was happening.

Bim, Doon and two others crept low through the floss to where they could see over a ridge whilst the others settled down silently to wait. Zig was disappointed not to be with his brothers but Bim had said it made sense for them to separate in case anything happened and he could see the logic of that.

From where they lay on their bellies, peeping over the ridge, the spies could see a very peaceful scene below them. They had obviously come to a thordite settlement and life seemed to be carrying on as normal.

They could see groups of thordite homes built from the wood of a shrub that the moogles didn't recognise. Small, irregular shacks stood around a clear area where youngsters played and elders gossiped. Many females could be seen going about their daily business and those watching were intrigued by a scene they had never looked upon before. They did notice that there didn't seem to be any males of working age and they decided to separate and scout around the perimeter to see if they could find where they might be.

Meeting back at the thicket a short while later, they had disappointingly little to report. They had found no groups of males, no sign of the missing moogles and Doon reported seeing the tracks of the carriage disappearing away from the far side of the settlement. After a brief discussion, they decided to make their way around the village in the gathering dusk and settle down for the night a short way along the track the other side.

Waiting for dusk, they managed to creep past the families of thordites (most now inside their homes for the night) without being seen and create a small collection of burrows in a mound of soft floss a little way off the path the far side. Setting up a rota of look-outs, they managed a reasonably comfortable night's sleep and, after a quick freshen up in the morning dew, they were on their way.

By late morning the atmosphere around them had changed. No one could quite say why but something was making them feel afraid. The floss was quite different now: hard and gritty under-foot and strange, unfamiliar shrubs grew much taller here than in their homelands, casting long, eerie shadows across their path. Yet there was also a change in the air around them making breathing more laboured and their fur stand on end.

A silent, unspoken agreement had them talking in whispers and only when necessary. They kept a careful lookout for activity as they moved slowly forward. No one knew what they expected to see at the end of their journey, but when they saw it, they all knew!

Creeping carefully, cautiously, around a curve in the track, they realised that they had reached their destination! Standing in front of them was the entrance to the most magnificent dwelling the moogles had ever seen and the tracks they had been following, swept straight in through the front entrance.

Moving hastily off the main path, the moogles gathered in a heavily shadowed area where they could hide yet have an undisturbed view of the palace; for that is what it must surely be. Speechlessly, they marvelled at what lay in front of them.

Rising up from the dull, grey floss was a building of such contrast it was breath-taking. The walls were made from some type of crystal (presumably the same as the carriage Blog had reported seeing) and it lit up the surrounding area as rays of sunlight danced from its smooth planes and bounced onto the ground around it. There were openings in the high walls that shone with the familiar blue of sapphires and the overall beauty of the building seemed to be in direct contrast with the drab, ugliness of its inhabitants, some of whom could be seen on guard at the front entrance and patrolling around its perimeter.

'Wow!' uttered Zig, echoing what they were all thinking.

'How are we ever going to get in there? It's an actual fortress!' whispered Doon.

'I have no idea at the moment, but we will!' answered Bim, with grim determination.

Moving a bit deeper into the wooded area, the group sat down to consider their options. It looked impossible to enter by the front door and not easy to take a look around in the daylight as the shadowed area they were now in seemed to be the only cover from the glaring light around the building. They were just discussing who would scout around the area after dark to see if there were any other entrances when Zig held up a paw to indicate silence and a hush fell over the group. Everyone listened carefully and, sure enough, a twig cracked a little way behind them.

Terrified that they were about to be discovered, yet unable to move in case they made a sound and gave away their position, the moogles sat frozen to the spot, looking in the direction the sound came from. Another sound, this time closer, and movement through the shadows, put fear into their hearts and they were just about to stand and fight when, into their circle came Raylee, Ressa and Zeeglit!

'Oh my, are we glad to see you!' exclaimed Bim.

'We couldn't believe it when we saw you arrive,' answered Raylee. 'We have been hiding here for a day now, wondering what to do. The place looks too well protected for three of us to attempt a rescue but now you are all here, we stand a chance.'

'How did you know where to come?' asked Zeeglit.

'When we arrived home, Blog told us the story of mother's capture and so we made our way back to the base camp to pick up the trail from there,' responded Doon. 'Have you seen anything since you've been here?'

'Nothing other than the sentries you can see and groups of thordite warriors coming and going occasionally. Did you have any problem getting home after the rescue?' continued Zeeglit.

'We certainly did!' Zig laughed and gave them a brief recount of what had happened.

Raylee looked rather shaken at the tale of the events and they agreed that they had been very lucky to make their escape safely. This refocused their thoughts on the safety of Pagloo and Froo and they set their minds to how they could attempt a rescue.

When the older moogles had arrived in the wooded area the day before, their thoughts had been similar to the younger group and so they had taken a good look around the crystal palace under the cover of darkness. They had discovered four more entrances around the building but each was watched by guards and they had not come up with any ideas on how to get in. The roof was too high to even begin to think about and the bright light around the perimeter would make it impossible to sneak up on the guards.

'Were all the entrances as heavily guarded?' asked one of the group: a heavily built, middle aged individual named Oxidly.

'No,' answered Zeeglit. 'The main entrance you can see now was definitely the most heavily protected and there was one small doorway with only two guards around the left-hand side of the building.'

'That might be our best chance,' suggested Zig.

'We could wait till the early hours and then rush them,' added Oxidly.

'I think we need daylight to be able to see once we're inside the palace,' said Raylee, thoughtfully. 'We don't know our way around or what we might find.'

'I don't see how we can get anywhere near the doorway. We'll be seen as soon as we leave the cover of the bushes.'

And so the discussion went on and the light began to fade. It was obvious they could do very little until morning but it was decided that Raylee would take Bim and Oxidly to see the quieter entrance when it got dark and the rest of the group would continue to think of a way in.

After sitting around, talking through ideas for a few hours and getting nowhere, the group lapsed into silence; a few moogles dozed off and the scouting party left to see what was happening at the side entrance.

Suddenly, Zeeglit sat up. 'I think I've got it!' he said. 'Yesterday morning, I was looking at the dimometer to see where we actually are, when it caught the light bouncing off the walls and I was worried we would be seen. The front face is made of crystal. We could use it to bounce the light back into the faces of the guards and sneak up on them.'

Sitting up with interest, Zig asked, 'How would we get them both?'

'We would have to be in a position to see when they were close together,' continued Zeeglit.

'They would see us before we got anywhere near enough for that,' said Doon.

There was a pause as the group considered this new possibility and then Zeeglit came up with another idea: 'What if we creep out when it's still dark and lie face-down in the floss, in full view of the palace, but using our coats for camouflage?'

'We'll be seen straight away!' argued Oxidly, horrified at the thought of being made a clear target.

'Not necessarily,' responded Zeeglit. 'They won't be expecting us to be there and our coats camouflage perfectly with the floss. If we settle well down and keep perfectly still, I don't think we will be seen.'

'It's crazy but it might just work and we need to do something,' said Zig.

By now, all those in the thicket were fully awake and talked in concerned whispers about Zeeglit's ideas. By the time Raylee and the others arrived back, the structure of the plan had been worked out and Zeeglit was able to explain it to them. Relieved to have a plan of action, Bim explained that there were still only two guards on the door and there were no windows overlooking the area so no one could be watching from above.

The problem of what to do about the guards when they got close was discussed at length: whilst moogles are a very peaceful species, this was war and they were determined to rescue their friends. The group of four who had attacked the warriors in the cavern were sure they could overpower two guards if they had the element of surprise on their side and Doon had noticed some strong creepers growing not far away which could be used to tie them up.

The next thing to do was work out what they would do when they got inside. As they had no idea of the layout of the palace or the whereabouts of Pagloo and Froo, there was little they could say, other than that they would split up into groups of three or four and head off in different directions.

They decided that they would sleep for a few hours, leaving one member of the group on guard. Cafeel volunteered for this as he had hurt his paw during the escape from the mines and he felt he might slow the others down. He would then wake the others just before dawn and they would slip out of hiding and find an uneven layer of floss where they could conceal themselves before the sun came up. Cafeel would stay hidden in the shadows in case the mission failed so that he could report back to the moogles at home and be able to lead another group to the palace if necessary.

Chapter 17
Inside the Palace

The moon was well hidden behind the Cirrostratus as the rescue party crept from their beds. Following Raylee's lead and keeping low, they made their way around to the left of the building until they could see the doorway. A few metres away, the floss was quite irregular and offered the perfect place for them to lie low.

Zeeglit, with the dimometer held tightly in his paw, nestled down nearest to the building, ready to deflect the sunlight. The four in the attack group came next, closely followed by another four, concealing lengths of creepers underneath them. By the time the first rays shone over the landscape, not a single creature could be seen and the guards began their day as normal.

For the moogles, lying on the damp floss, the wait seemed endless. They could only hope that they were camouflaged from above and that Zeeglit's plan would work. They had agreed that they would leave it up to Zeeglit to judge when the time was right and he would give a quiet whistle when he was about to start.

Listening carefully and trying not to move a muscle, the moogles waited. They could feel the warmth on their backs as the sun climbed higher in the sky and they heard the guards talking to one another as they changed shifts but no-one seemed to notice their presence. Then they heard the low whistle they had been waiting for.

Everyone moved at once: Zeeglit lifted his hand and twisted the dimometer until the rays of the sun bounced from its face and then swivelled it until it was pointing in the direction of the guards. As their exclamations of surprise reached the moogles' ears, the first wave of the assault was already flowing across the floss behind Zeeglit and the four strong, confident adults from the cavern attack easily overpowered the guards.

In no time, they were bound tightly and hidden from view. Doon had thought to bring handfuls of leaves which were pushed into their mouths to prevent them shouting for help and the whole party had squeezed inside the small entrance hall. Keeping silent and using gestures, they decided on the directions they would take and small groups slipped off into the great palace.

From the side porch, corridors led off to the left and right and a larger hallway lay straight in front of them. This space was the largest they had ever seen inside a dwelling and it appeared to have very little purpose. The crystal walls glowed with reflected light coming from some kind of lamps hanging at regular intervals around the edge which flickered and shone but did not use the glow worms familiar to moogles. The floor was covered with creepers, similar to those used to restrain the guards, woven into large mats and across the other side of this, they could see steps leading upward: a very strange scene indeed for moogles who live their lives in burrows under the ground and had never seen a staircase before! The steps were wide and shallow with gaps between each tread and a few of the visitors thought they looked terrifying.

Keeping close to the walls, with eyes and ears wide open, the groups began their search for the captives. Two groups disappeared down the passages to either side and the rest made their way swiftly across the hallway. A further two groups made their way, with great trepidation, up the steps and the final two headed towards the two doorways they could see leading off from the hallway.

Zeeglit, Ressa, Zig, Doon and Oxidly were in one of the groups that began to climb the stairs, very keen to see what happened at the top! The stairway curved back on itself and finished in another open space like the one below. The sounds of voices and activity came from both sides of the building and they were obviously in danger of being seen if they stayed where they were. Quickly, the two groups parted company and headed towards two identical archways at either side of the hallway. Zeeglit led his group to one side of their entrance and indicated that they should stay well back against the wall. Moving very cautiously, he edged along until he could just peep around and see what lay through the opening.

The area that he was looking into was breath-taking and he knew immediately that they had found their goal yet their troubles were certainly not over yet!

One massive room covered a whole side of the building and was crawling with thordites going about assorted activities. Some were sitting around talking whilst others were quietly relaxing on a comfortable nest of catilly grass. The group nearest to Zeeglit were working on some unfamiliar type of machine and several guards seemed to be keeping a lookout through the stunning blue windows: slabs of sapphire, cut so thin as to be transparent. All this, he took in in an instant, yet it was the activity at the front end of the room that drew Zeeglit's attention.

There seemed to be a high-level meeting taking place with several imposing looking thordites arguing and Isilit, herself, presiding over the proceedings. Tempers were running high although from this distance, Zeeglit could not make out what was being said though it was pretty clear what the subject of the discussions was: hanging from the ceiling in the centre of the arena were two cages, woven from creepers, housing Pagloo and Froo.

Although some distance away, he could see that both moogles seemed to be in good health as they were standing and seemed to be following the proceedings. Ducking back into the hallway, he quickly told the others what he had seen. They decided that Zig would take over the position in the doorway to see if he could hear what was going on as his hearing was particularly sensitive.

It didn't take him long to get the gist of it and what he reported back to the others made grim hearing. It appeared that they had arrived in time to hear the trial of the only two moogles that had been captured from the raid at the mines and most of the thordites were determined to make an example of them: holding them responsible for all that had happened at the caverns.

Whilst he was telling the group this, they were joined by two of the other groups from downstairs who had found nothing except a few off-duty guards and a kitchen where a meal was being prepared.

However, the other group from upstairs also arrived with a very interesting tale. They had looked into several empty rooms and one with a few warriors relaxing before finding a very grand suite of living rooms at the back of the palace that they assumed belonged to the ruler herself. Making their way through the suite, they had come to a beautiful, quiet sleeping chamber where a young female kept watch over what seemed to be a very sick young thordite.

Zig, who had crept back to the doorway to gather what he could, reappeared looking very concerned. It appeared that the angry individuals addressing the meeting had been in the caverns when the rescue had taken place and were putting a strong case against Pagloo and Froo. It was no surprise to Zeeglit to learn that Isilit had no sympathy for the moogles and there were shouts for them to be thrown from the Stratus.

Zeeglit joined Zig at the archway to assess what could be done as another group of four from downstairs joined the band of moogles waiting in the corridor. It appeared that some sort of decision was about to be made as Isilit stood up. She raised her arms for silence and an instant hush fell over the gathering.

'All that I need to hear has been said. I have no doubt that these two are not the main architects of the plan to destroy our mines but they were part of the mission and an example must be set. They will be taken from here at sundown and thrown from the Stratus. Their tunics will be delivered to their homeland to show their people that we mean business.'

'You will never defeat the moogles with wickedness!' Pagloo's voice could be heard clearly from where her son was listening and he felt tears spring to his eyes. A slight movement behind told them that Raylee and Ressa had joined them and, without taking time to discuss or think things through, Zeeglit jumped to his feet.

To the amazement of his father and friends, he began to stride towards the trial as quickly as his short legs would take him. Nevertheless, he didn't get very far before he was pounced on by warriors and hauled down to Isilit.

A few minutes of confusion followed. Not sure what Zeeglit had been about to do, the moogles were initially unsure whether to follow or remain hidden but two warriors coming up the stairs behind them sent them scurrying into the room after Zeeglit. There was a great uproar amongst the inhabitants of the grand chamber as the foreigners were overpowered and shepherded to the front and Pagloo could be heard above it all, shouting for her family.

Once again, Isilit raised her arms and quiet reigned. Virtually shaking with fury, she turned her full attention on Zeeglit and in a voice dripping with venom she uttered the single word: 'YOU!'

'That is right,' came the reply and his friends were surprised to hear that his voice was steady.

'You dare to come to my home. Surely you did not think you could avoid capture and you knew that you would not escape if our paths ever crossed again. What did you expect to gain?'

'When I left the mine, I certainly hoped never to see you again. However, we look after our families and friends and we have come to take these two home,' said Zeeglit, indicating Pagloo and Froo, swaying in their cages a few metres above the proceedings.

When the unpleasant laughter of the thordite warriors died down, Isilit asked the question that was also on the lips of the moogles present: 'Why on earth would we let you walk away from here?'

'Because we have something that you need,' came the simple answer.

'What can I possibly need that you can provide?' she asked; obviously puzzled.

'Well,' said Zeeglit, the whole room hanging on his every word and at a loss to know what was going to come next, 'I happen to know that your offspring is very ill. As Blauron would tell you, my father is able to heal.'

Those standing close to Isilit noticed her flinch, otherwise she gave nothing away. 'What makes you think that is the case?' she asked.

'I just know. We can heal your youngster if you are prepared to let all our people walk free. We don't want any trouble and we will never come to this place again. We just want to go home and carry on with our ordinary lives.'

'I have heard enough. I will speak with my council.' And turning to one side she commanded, 'Guards, watch them. If any of them move, kill them!' She then swept from the great chamber, followed by the members of the council including Blauron, and the moogles were pushed into a corner and made to sit whilst the guards watched them and whispered to one another.

'Are you crazy?' asked Oxidly. 'What did you think you were doing?'

Having worked out what his friend was up to, Zig responded. 'Trust him. Zeeglit knows what he is doing.'

'Well, I think he's going to get us all killed,' Oxidly replied anxiously.

Meanwhile, Raylee had managed to have a quick word with his partner before the guards stopped him and the boys were able to reassure themselves that their mother was indeed unharmed. Doon had also told Froo that they would not leave here without her and they could do nothing else but wait for the verdict of the council.

After what seemed an age, the council reappeared and the group waited to hear their fate. Once they were all settled, Isilit began to give their verdict.

'I once made it very clear that if I ever saw you again it would not end well for you. However, we have discussed your proposition and there may be room for negotiation although I need some answers from you first. How did you know I have a youngster that is unwell?'

'Some of our party saw the little one in its bed and reported back to me. It was obvious it was yours because the suite of rooms was unlikely to belong to anyone else.'

They saw Isilit visibly flinch as Zeeglit mentioned that moogles had actually been able to reach the bedroom and it was obvious that she was very concerned about her youngster.

'Blauron has told me about the way your father helped his foolish daughter and we have long known about the healing power of some moogles. Where is your father now?'

'I'm here,' said Ressa quietly as he moved to stand beside his son.

'Whilst I have heard tales of bones and bruises being healed, I have not heard whether you can heal sickness,' said Isilit.

Speaking directly to Isilit, to address her concerns as a mother, Ressa tried to reassure her: 'The gift I have is not selective. I don't know why I am able to heal but I know that I can. As you say, bruises and broken bones are easy to heal whilst sickness is less so. If you just let me try, I am sure I can make your little one better.'

There was a pause for a few moments as she spoke with two officials behind her (one of whom was Blauron) and then she turned back.

'You and your son will come with me,' she announced haughtily. 'We will see if you have the ability to free your people.'

'No, I won't,' Ressa replied.

'I beg your pardon? I thought you said you would cure my daughter.'

'I said I would cure your youngster *if* you agreed to let my people leave this place and return home.'

'How dare you question me?' snapped Isilit.

'Because I need to know that you will set us free if I do this for you.'

'Agreed,' she snapped. 'Now come with me.'

'Once you have let these two out of their cages,' bargained Ressa.

Turning to the two guards nearest the prisoners, she snarled, 'Do it! Now you come with me.' And with blue robes trailing, she swept past the group and headed off down the room. Ressa and Zeeglit, escorted by two guards, followed.

Making their way across the landing and through the opposite doorway, the moogles hurried to keep up. They passed several rooms before they reached Isilit's private apartment at the back of the palace. Still they continued until they came to the bedroom. Instructing the guards to remain outside the door, she beckoned the others to follow her inside.

The nursemaid leapt to her feet as her mistress entered the room and she looked shocked as the elderly moogle and his son followed her. Ressa crossed to the bed and looked down at the young female who appeared to be about five years old and very obviously unwell. Her complexion was very pale and her breathing was erratic. Turning to her mother he asked,

'How long has she been like this?'

'When we returned from the mines, I was told she had fallen ill some days before. I fear she is getting worse every day. Can you help?' This was no longer a powerful leader but a concerned parent and Ressa responded accordingly.

'I think I can. Do I have your word that we can go free?'

'Yes, if my daughter revives.'

Without another word, Ressa stretched out his paws and very gently placed them either side of the youngster's head. Closing his eyes, he appeared to go into a kind on trance and Isilit watched with fascinated hope. After a few minutes Ressa straightened and looked at Isilit.

'Your daughter is very sick and I'm not sure my powers are strong enough.'

Wordlessly, Zeeglit rounded the far side of the bed and stood opposite his father. Reaching out his paws, he placed them on top of his fathers. Ressa seemed to understand and together father and son spread a warm blanket of healing over the youngster.

This process lasted a few minutes but the warm glow faded and they lifted their paws. At first there was nothing but then they saw her eyelids begin to flutter. Ressa moved back to allow Isilit to get close to her daughter and he could have sworn there were tears in the great leader's eyes as her daughter blinked, twice then looked clearly into her mother's face and smiled.

As she scooped her up into a close embrace, Ressa beckoned Zeeglit and they tiptoed quietly from the room where they waited with the guards. After a short while, Isilit joined them. She had regained her composure but she turned to Ressa and Zeeglit, looking them directly in the eyes, she said,

'Thank you. You have given me the most precious gift.' Then, turning on her heel, she led the way back into the main hall where the others were waiting; Pagloo and Froo standing with the others.

'Let them go,' she commanded the guards. 'Escort them to the far side of our lands and watch them go on their way. May this be an end to things between us.' And, without a backward glance, she headed off back down the room; Ressa suspected, to return to her daughter.

Without waiting to be asked twice, the moogles hurried along between the guards. As they made their way down the great staircase, they memorised the details to tell their families when they got home: such a sight they would remember for ever! Across the main hall, this time they passed through the main doorway before breathing the fresh air many had never thought to breathe again.

As instructed, the guards followed the quiet group along the path until they had passed the settlement they'd seen on their way until, suddenly, Zig said, 'Look!' and looking back, they realised that their escort was no longer with them. Then conversation and celebration began in earnest!

Finally, the group realised they were free and life felt good. Pagloo, Raylee and their sons laughed and hugged and Zeeglit and Ressa were praised and clapped on the back. Turning for home, they chattered and laughed and relived their adventure as they made their way gaily along the track. It was almost dark by the time they reached home but they were determined to get back on familiar ground before they settled down for the night.

A few of their neighbours were awake as they came towards the burrows and it wasn't long before many more had gathered in the central clearing to hear their tale: illuminated by the warmth of many glow lamps, it made a very colourful picture and it was the wee small hours before many moogles got to sleep that night!

Chapter 18
A Time to Celebrate

Waking in Raylee's family burrow the following morning, Zeeglit felt good. No more loose ends; no more worries; no more reasons to delay going home. Stretching out on his comfortable mattress of catilly grass, he though over the last few months and knew he was ready to go home. He spent some time thinking about his family at home and wondered if they had missed him as much as he had missed them and, with a feeling of excitement, he made his way outside for his morning grooming session.

However, once he came out into the fresh air, it seemed as if the area was awash with moogles rushing about with equal excitement. Spotting Zig a short way off, he made his way over.

'Hi-lo. What's happening?' he asked.

'There's to be a great party tonight. Word has reached many other communities and they are all to come together here tonight to celebrate our great victory.'

When Zeeglit explained his desire to go home, Zig quickly assured him he couldn't and dragged him over to Ressa who was helping to set up some catilly mattresses around the perimeter of the meeting place. His father was in no doubt that they must stay as they were to be the guests of honour and, after all this time, one more day would make little difference. Seeing no way around it, Zeeglit went to freshen up before doing what he could to help in the preparations.

Food was being gathered and prepared along one side of the clearing and there seemed to be quite a range of specialities on offer. Zeeglit could see evidence of mimberries, giving their undeniable colour to several dishes and there were other goodies that he had never seen before. Beginning to feel hungry, he concentrated on the lighting he was helping Zig and Bim to prepare. Glow lamps, in a variety of shades, would be hung around the festivities and the boys were responsible for putting up posts to hang them on.

Doon and Froo were helping to make a stage at one edge of the clearing, from which there would be entertainment and speeches. It was made from blocks of floss cut from a cliff face not far away and stored in the neighbourhood for community events. The blocks were carried from their storage area, put into position and secured with pegs carved from the trunk of the Altotuft shrubs.

The day flew past and Zeeglit had little time to think about home. He did, however, have time to realise how much he would miss his new friends and hoped that, one day, they would be able to visit him so he could introduce them to his family and show them the same hospitality they had shown him.

As the light began to fade at the end of the day, moogles began streaming into the square and the colourful glow lamps lit up their happy faces. Zeeglit came from the burrow and wandered over to where his father was sitting talking with Raylee.

'Well, my friend; what adventures we have had! I feel as if I have known you all my life and I know we have you and your son to thank for so many things. You will make a wonderful role model for my boys to follow and we will all miss you dreadfully,' said Raylee.

Feeling very choked up, Ressa put his arm around his friend's shoulder and gave him a hug. They were soon joined by the rest of the family and, side by side, they sat and enjoyed the festivities. They were entertained by a group of musicians playing a type of whistle carved from the woody stems of various shrubs. The density of the wood and the varying lengths of the whistles created a variety of sound that blended to give a tuneful melody. The music they played was merry and many moogles were dancing in the centre of the clearing whilst those sat around the edge had a job to keep their feet from tapping in time to the beat.

The feast was magnificent and they all felt that they wouldn't want to eat again for days!

Zeeglit thought about the ice-cirrus and mimberries that he had safely stored in his pack inside the burrow and once again his thoughts turned towards home and the thrill he would have as his family tasted these unusual flavours. He also wondered if the return of the star to the heavens would make their crop of tuft return to its healthy state and could only hope so.

As the evening wore on, many moogles he had never even met came to thank him and his father for all they had done to help their community. Ressa was very pleased to see the locals he had helped to heal, out and enjoying their health and the company of their youngsters who had been taken from them. For a moment, he wondered how the young thordite was doing and, despite their aggressive nature, he was glad he had been able to help.

It was round about the midnight hour when there was a break in the music and Raylee made his way up onto the stage. As he called for attention, a hush fell over the gathering and all eyes turned towards him.

'My friends,' he began. 'What a time we have had!' Waiting for the sounds of agreement to die down, he continued: 'For a while, I thought our darkest days had come and I was in despair of ever seeing two of my sons again. Then our friends Ressa and Zeeglit came back to visit. To be blessed with the gift of healing is a wonderful thing and Ressa has certainly put it to good use recently. I, for one, will always be grateful.

'From now on, we will always be wary of possible danger from the thordites, but I don't think they will be bothering us any time soon. We have Ressa and Zeeglit to thank for the rescue of all the captives from the mines and also for saving Pagloo and Froo from the palace.'

Reaching behind him, Raylee took two small packages from Bim who was standing just off the stage. 'Ressa, Zeeglit, can I ask you to come up and accept a small token of our appreciation.'

Feeling rather overcome with emotion, the heroes of the moment stood and made their way through a gap that appeared in the crowd, towards their friend, standing on the stage.

'Come up. Come up here, friends,' he said, reaching down to pull Zeeglit up onto the stage as Ressa climbed the steps. A great cheer rang out from the crowd as they turned to face them and Raylee presented them both with a package, carefully wrapped in the softest bru-floss leaves. Moving them carefully aside, Zeeglit gently pulled out a stunningly beautiful waistcoat. It was woven in white, shot with strands of silver and a band of dark grey stitching ran around the edges. It was the most beautiful one he had ever seen and for a moment he was too choked for words, though he did manage to change into the new garment and it fitted perfectly.

Looking across to his father, he could see Ressa also wearing an equally impressive waistcoat and looking quite overcome. Coughing gently to clear his throat, Ressa uttered a gruff, 'Thank you all so much,' which was echoed by Zeeglit before another huge cheer rang out and both moogles were hoisted onto the shoulders of several strong males and paraded round the meeting place.

Shortly afterwards, the party began to break up and those moogles from further away made their way homewards. Sitting, once again, with the family, Ressa thanked them sincerely for the gifts and asked where they had come from.

It appeared that there was a talented weaver living not too far away and, whilst everyone had been busy preparing for the party during the day, Raylee and Pagloo had slipped away to select the gifts. They had said they wanted something special and when she knew who it was for, the weaver showed them a piece of fabric she had been saving for a special occasion.

It had been created from the hair of a very unusual albino moogle, mixed with silver strands from the coat of a dansue: a very rare creature indeed, that spends most of its life burrowed under the deepest layers of floss. They had agreed that it would be ideal for the waistcoat and she had suggested that she embroidered around the edge using some grey thread taken from the coats of moogle babies, making it particularly fine and shiny.

The completed item had arrived just before the celebrations and everyone had felt it was perfect. Zeeglit had to agree and he was sure that he would never again see such a fine item. The fit was perfect and he smiled as he thought what his mother would say when she saw it.

Eventually, the last of the families drifted away to bed and Zeeglit made his way back to his sleeping chamber for the last time. Folding his new waistcoat carefully, he placed it in his pack for the journey home the next day and lay down on his soft mattress.

The first half of the following day was spent clearing up from the day before and the afternoon was a lazy one, spent lolling around; dozing and chatting in the central chamber of the burrow. Neighbours dropped in during the day to wish the travellers well and details of the adventures were taken out and picked over again and again. No one felt much like eating, having stuffed themselves at the party, but they did manage a small meal late in the afternoon as they waited for the sky to darken before Ressa and Zeeglit could make their way to the moonbeam port.

Although both father and son couldn't wait to get home to see their family, it was with heavy hearts that farewells were made, early that evening. All the family had gathered at the entrance to the burrow to see them on their way and Ressa and Zeeglit hauled their heavy packs onto their backs before making their way through the scene of the previous night's festivities. They headed back in the direction of the nearest port and the route home, having made their hosts promise to journey to the lower level to meet the rest of the family in the not-too-distant future.

Activity at the port was brisk and Zeeglit took his place beside his father to wait for the beams to appear. Luckily it was a clear night and before too long, they stepped into a strong shaft and made their way downward.

As they sank lower, Zeeglit's mind travelled back over all his experiences since he'd left home a few months earlier and he chuckled as he thought of how he would tell his family of his adventures, though the sight of those first thordite warriors standing over him would remain in his mind for a long time.

The descent was uneventful and, as they left the shaft at the port on the Nimbo-stratus, Zeeglit felt a rush of excitement. The air at this level was several degrees warmer and there was a familiar smell that he had never really noticed before but which settled round him: comfortable and safe, like a favourite blanket.

Feeling wide awake and more confident now he was on familiar territory, Zeeglit was happy to continue on his way for a few hours. He whistled a tune as he walked alongside his father across the denser floss of the Nimbo-Stratus, noticing small details of the landscape around him and cherishing the feeling of coming home. Finally, not able to keep going any longer, Zeeglit was glad to help Ressa scoop out a shallow burrow and curl up to sleep together through the hours until dawn.

The following morning dawned fresh and bright. As they sat grooming their fur, Zeeglit gazed at highlights of gold where the sun's rays penetrated the Altostratus and bounced off the pure white floss before him. Then, with a spring in his step, he set off on the final leg of his journey.

Exhausted yet excited, Zeeglit paused as he climbed over the last mound of floss before reaching his home. His journey had been long and tiring and he was looking forward to being surrounded by the love and warmth always present in his family burrow. Whilst hard, the trip had been fulfilling and he knew how excited his family would be to see the treasures he and his father had strapped to their backs. He did wonder for a moment about the reception he would get from his mother as he had run away from home at the start of the adventure but it was such a bright and exciting morning, he soon forgot about it.

The soft, uneven mounds of floss shone gently in the early morning sunlight and Zeeglit could just make out the Burrows of Snay in the distance. As if he could read his mind, Ressa asked, 'Ready?'

With his family so close, Zeeglit nodded, readjusted his pack and, with a lift in his step and a smile on his face, began the homeward stretch.

Meanwhile, Augil, sitting outside their burrow watching their youngest, Exie, playing on the floss, jumped to her feet as she made out the figures of Ressa and Zeeglit coming towards her.

Ressa looked tired from his journey but she could see from his expression and the stoop of his shoulders that his mission had been a success and she stood to wait for them.